FUCK YOUR

FEELINGS

Get to Work

Sajad Abid Husain, Esq.

Cover designed by Jen Carpenter

Sajad Abid Husain, Esq.
Visit my website at www.causeandeffectconsulting.com

Printed in the United States of America

First Printing: October 2014
Amazon/KDP

ISBN-13 9798344909660

I would like to thank me for always being me and for failing at killing myself four times in my twenties.

Thank you to my former clients, who are now my friends, and my other friends, who contributed to this manual.

Thanks to Jen as well, even though she charged me money.

Thank you to my mother for being so loving and to my father for making me into a man, instead of a fucking pussy.

- Sajad Abid Husain, Esq

CONTENTS

WHAT OTHERS SAY ABOUT SAJAD

"If you make one decision today, it should be to read this manual and then hire Sajad! And when you do, listen to him…..He will cut to the chase and not waste your time. He will help you streamline your thinking and cut out the mental clutter. If you lack focus, he will help you figure that out. Consider him a paid professional truth teller.

This manual will be an excellent first step in getting to know how he thinks and works…then buckle up and get ready for a ride that will take you to a new and better place. I have met a lot of interesting people in my life and work and he is the number one most impactful person I have ever met. If you don't take action, perhaps you should ask yourself, "what are you waiting for?" Just do it."

-Daryl B. Shankland, President of Shankland Financial Advisors, LLC Over 4 decades of creativity on Wall Street

"In the maze of modern productivity and self-improvement, Sajad Abid Husain, Esq emerges as a beacon of massive value. Sajad unveils the journey of a leader who defies convention at every turn. Known for his controversial stance and autonomous approach, Sajad is more than a productivity coach; he is a visionary, challenging the very fabric of personal and professional growth.

To the untrained eye, he presents an enigma—self-sufficient, seemingly detached, yet at his core lies a fiercely loyal heart, dedicated to forging deep, meaningful connections. Sajad's philosophy is not for the faint-hearted. It demands courage, an unwavering commitment to truth, and the readiness to confront one's deepest self.

His methods, distilled from years of mastering the art of productivity, are transformative, offering not just strategies for making more money, but a radical new way of living and thinking. This manual is a testament to his genius, a guide for those daring enough to seek authenticity and excellence.

If you're ready to challenge your limits and embrace radical honesty, let Sajad Abid Husain, Esq lead you to a future where success is not just measured by wealth, but by the depth of your connections and the authenticity of your journey.

Dive into **FUCK YOUR FEELINGS GET TO WORK**, and discover how to harness your true potential, guided by one of the most brilliant minds in the realm of personal development."

-Suzanne Taylor-King MCPC, CHLC, CaPP, Founder of Taylord Coaching

Sometimes the thing that is holding you back...

is all in your head.

PREFACE

Are you ready to get shit done?

I only care about your success, not your excuses.

If you want to succeed without having to live through the fiery trials I've been through, then you need tough love. The experiences I've had make me the perfect person to give you that.

Do you want someone to feel sorry for you? That's not me.

Do you want to get to know me better and hear more of my story?

Well, you won't.

Not until I teach you how to make money and live the life you've always wanted, then and only then can we be friends. Maybe.

Along with my dog, Sweets, I'm living life exactly the way I want and helping my clients make a ton of money.

Are you ready to learn from an expert who doesn't care about your lame excuses but will make sure you have everything you need to get shit done?

This manual is derived from the exact online course of my six-week business coaching boot camp program. These timeless yet simple principles of sales, business, mindset, and entrepreneurship only work when you follow my expertise 100%.

You must forget about everything you were doing before because it wasn't working. Follow this program exactly as it is laid out, because it is a proven system, and it works. If you "do it kind of your way", it won't work at all.

You must stick strictly to the program.

In many ways, the messages of *FUCK YOUR FEELINGS GET TO WORK,* are the hard facts of truth, reality, and honesty by blaming yourself for everything to grow and change. Readers can expect that I will be raw and real as I have rocked more than a few boats through my teachings over the years.

Will you cry at some point? Probably.
Will you laugh at times? YES!
Will you be glad you bought this manual? 100%, if you follow it.
FUCK YOUR FEELINGS! GET TO WORK...

- Shows people exactly how to run and grow a successful business through organization, productivity, planning, providing massive value, and taking consistent intentional action
- Challenges the belief that spending time reading, researching, creating, and analyzing are productive income-producing activities
- Teaches you how to clearly and concisely articulate massive value, understand return on investment and customer acquisition costs, map out a solid plan, and master skills in negotiations and closing
- Explodes the myth that you need to run "get to know you" meetings instead of structured business meetings when networking
- Defines the entrepreneurial mentality required to sustain what it takes to grow a thriving business and live a more fulfilling life

Cause and Effect Consulting is changing the world!

By becoming extremely well organized, you will significantly increase your productivity and substantially reduce your stress.

Everything is your fucking fault.

-Sajad Abid Husain, Esq

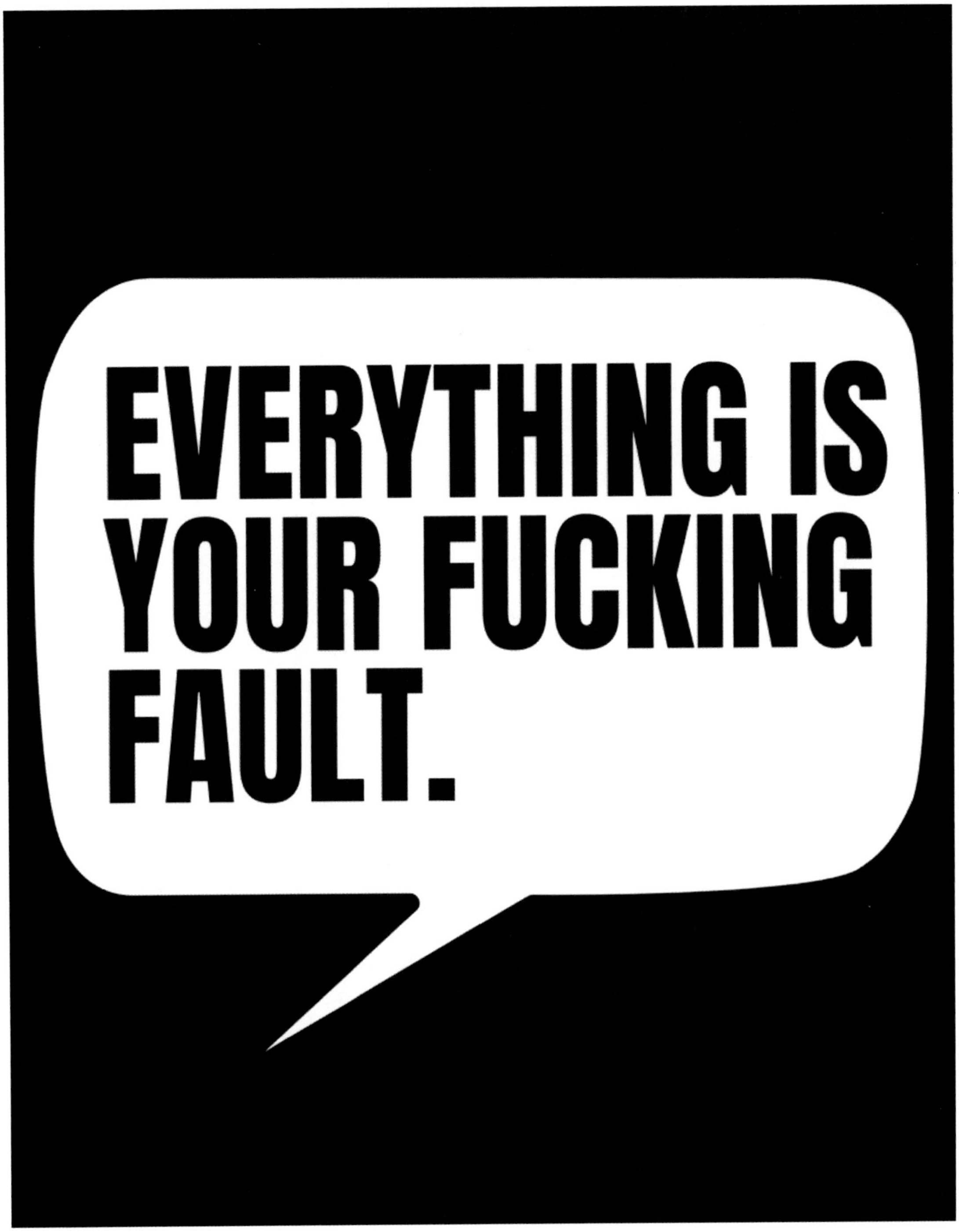
EVERYTHING IS YOUR FUCKING FAULT.

INTRODUCTION: LET'S FUCKING GO!

How to Develop a Schedule

BE THE PIMP AND NOT THE WHORE.

What matters is creating wealth and having autonomy; to be free from external forces.

To do whatever you want, whenever you want.

The only way to get there is to do the opposite of the victim; the victim blames others and external forces for their current condition and position.

An autonomous man understands that it's all about self-accountability; you only create, gain, and possess power, by being hyper self-critical, without taking it personally.

Everything is your fucking fault.

This is all about taking control of your business and your life.

Be the pimp and not the whore.

Do NOT skip ahead and get ahead of the program.

Follow exactly what is laid out in this manual. It is a proven system and only works when you listen to and do exactly what it says.

Here is how to develop your schedule.

You probably don't have a good understanding of how much work you are actually getting done. Activity does not equal productivity.

Being busy is not productive and you're probably lying to yourself saying, "I am working 12 hours a day."

Most people work between three and five hours per day.

Really, you are just busy doing things that are not income-producing activities and wasting precious   time.

Here are things that don't make money right away:

- Researching,
- reading,
- creating,
- analyzing, etc.

Do these things instead:

1. Go to networking events.
2. Pitch (to pitch means to concisely and clearly articulate massive value) your business to as many people as possible.
3. Get your calendar filled up (a lot more on this later).
4. Close deals (a lot more on this later).

Stop fucking bullshitting yourself. You're fucking scared.

You do not start out with confidence, you start out with courage; the courage to try.

You fail and fail and fail.

As you learn, you develop confidence. You don't start out with confidence. You start out with the courage to try.

Run into discomfort; let yourself become extremely uncomfortable; muscles grow, after they rip. Get out there. Make yourself fucking famous. Love your haters. Thank them.

How do you ensure that you are actually getting shit done?

This is what a sample schedule looks like.

Created by Orrin Lieuwen lionheartleadership.ca

Date: _____ ⏱ + =

Work Time	Time Slots	Activities & Outcomes Planned		What went wrong & learnings	
	5:00-5:30				
	5:30-6:00				
	6:00-6:30				
	6:30-7:00				
	7:00-7:30				
	7:30-8:00				
	8:00-8:30				
	8:30-9:00				
	9:00-9:30				
	9:30-10:00				
	10:00-10:30				
	10:30-11:00				
	11:00-11:30				
	11:30-12:00				
	12:00-12:30				
	12:30-1:00				
	1:00-1:30				
	1:30-2:00				
	2:00-2:30				
	2:30-3:00				
	3:00-3:30				
	3:30-4:00				
	4:00-4:30				
	4:30-5:00				
	5:00-5:30				
	5:30-6:00				
	6:00-6:30				
	6:30-7:00				
	7:00-7:30				
	7:30-8:00				
	8:00-8:30				
	8:30-9:00				

Here put your mission that inspires, you, and attitudes you need to cultivate day to day.

Notice Everything.   Celebrate your wins
   Take responsibility for everything that goes wrong. Learn, then celebrate your learning.

In a 24-hour period, you will have a twelve-hour work schedule, you get four hours off, and you'll get eight hours of sleep.

The day before, you will take 30-60 minutes to **hand write** your detailed and specific work schedule activities with quantifiable measurements, intentions, and clear, quantifiable outcomes in addition to break times and personal time.

With time and practice, you will be able to get this done in 15 minutes.
Through this process, you will discover what is actually getting done and why you are not getting things done in a 12-hour workday within the days and forthcoming weeks of this process.

On the left side of your schedule, you will add up your working hours to total up to 12 working hours.
Next, you will list a detailed description of each of the tasks, line by line, one at a time, with specific and quantifiable measurements, intention, and the confirmed outcomes. You will schedule your personal time and leisure time as well so you know exactly where you are putting your time and energy.
You will find that, at the end of the day, your schedule may not be going as planned.
As you are working throughout the day, you will find that not everything is getting done. Why? It is usually for one of a few reasons so you may consider developing a notation system.
For example, you might put a red X where the specific work task went overboard because you underestimated how much time it took to complete, you made an error in scheduling, you allowed yourself to get distracted, lost focus, or got side tracked by shiny object syndrome.

This is how things don't get done.

Stick strictly to the schedule, you will get better and better at this every day. It's like a diet or a budget; it doesn't mean shit if you don't stick to it.

For example, you plan on attending a one-hour networking event:

- *Are you doing your 30-second pitch or your 1-2-minute pitch?*

- *How many people will you be pitching?*

- *How many people do you expect to get on your calendar for a 1:1 conversation business meeting?*

- *How many people do you intend to email or direct message on social media to get three people on your calendar?*

There's a big difference between saying, "attend networking event" and the actual activity related to your intention and expected outcome in this example.

SET A CLEAR, QUANTIFIABLE GOAL FOR EACH LINE.

Yes, I'm yelling.

Every day, you will be learning new things about where you are spending your time and where you are not being productive.

MULTITASKING IS DOING TWO THINGS WRONG AT THE SAME TIME.

At the end of the day, there are really a few reasons for an issue with a task.

On your schedule, you can use "L" lag. What does that mean? That means that if you were supposed to start a task at 1:00 PM and you started that task at 1:10 PM, then you were lagging, and you lost 10 minutes of your time.

Take a look at what came before it and correct this on the next day.

Surprise!!!! Things like breaks and lunchtime, going for a walk, or taking an unplanned phone call tend to cause lag.

We tell ourselves things are an emergency when they are not. It is all about respecting and valuing your own time and doing the same for other people.

You have been setting really low expectations for yourself. Your standards of what can get done in a day are bullshit.

You keep going down rabbit holes and chasing squirrels.

You lack self-discipline. You need to really, be your own boss.

Also, don't overwhelm yourself. Do not create unrealistic expectations for what can get done in a day.

Just be fucking honest.

Stick strictly to the schedule; stop fucking lying to yourself.

DON'T THINK. JUST DO.

When you have something like a scheduled 30-minute pitch/business meeting or you are going to meet with a client in person, don't schedule going for a walk beforehand or go over time on your scheduled meeting and take away time dedicated for your next set of scheduled business tasks.

It is extremely beneficial and important to understand the psychology behind why things are getting done and not getting done.

The next outcome might be marked with an "X" for incomplete. And this most likely means you under allocated time. A question mark means the task was too vague.

If the work task is something like, "work on your website", that is very vague.

If I put, "complete the header banner section on my website", that is more specific. You will learn how to break your tasks down into exact steps through this scheduling process.

One task might actually need to be broken down into three or five steps.

Back to the example of working on the banner for your website…

- **Step one** is to upload my picture into the banner image.
- **Step two** is to update the copy on the banner.
- **Step three** is to do the designing, formatting, polishing, and uploading of the final image to your website.

What you thought was one task on your schedule, you will learn that it may need to be broken down into three tasks.

Quite often, you will learn and write a little arrow on your schedule to move a task to a different place in your schedule, as it means there was a dependency issue. Completing one task may be dependent on the other…

At 4:00 PM, you planned to work on your profile picture and banner image, and at 2:00 PM you planned to add the image to your website. You will have to do one task before the other so you will learn exactly where you are messing things up.

By making these annotations, it reveals our tendency to lag on certain things and when we are being too vague with our tasks. What you will end up doing from now on is thinking more about project management.

Back to the website task again. You will lay out the exact steps and components required to complete the task and put how long I think it's going to take.

Will it take thirty minutes or sixty minutes?

Now, you will put these activities into the appropriate time slots, and you are much more clear on exactly what you are going to be doing in your detailed schedule for the next day.

This is the basis of how to manage your scheduling system. Block out and schedule the time, add up the hours, check your outcomes at the end of the day, and then lay out more specific tasks for the following days.

Also, you can jot down notes at the bottom or on the back of your schedule as you go about your day for tasks that will need to be added to your schedule the next day.

Keep a notebook and pen with you to write things down throughout your day.

Putting a pen to paper gets things out of your head and by doing this you will cause yourself less stress and feel less overwhelmed as you move forward with your scheduling process every day.

STICK STRICTLY TO THE SCHEDULE: No rabbit holes, no shiny objects, no dumb ass excuses.

Spending one hour a day creating your schedule for the next day will cause you to be at least four times more productive the next day if you stick strictly to the schedule.

Abundance vs Scarcity --Limited Availability

Do not have more than two days open on your Calendly.

- If you do, it shows that you're desperate for money AND/OR it shows that you ain't got shit going on. It's best that your upcoming schedule is already blocked out— even if YOU have to block it out.
- If things are 3 or 4 weeks blocked out—GREAT. It shows that your time is very valuable and that you must have your shit going on.

Your potential client will understand that.

- They'll email you saying—I have to wait?
- You say, "Did you want to hire me?"
  - If they say "yes", **YOU HAVE TIME NOW**. Don't say some BS like "someone just canceled". Just say "I have time right now."

CHAPTER ONE: BRANDING, PITCHING, PACKAGES, AND PROCESSES

The first thing you need to do is have an emotional connection in your pitch.

Why do you need to make an emotional connection in your pitch?

People buy into the subconscious based on emotion. They don't buy based on logic.

If you say what you do and how you do it, you're not resonating in the person's mind in the way that you need to for the way that they are going to decide whether they buy or not.

An emotional connection is how you make somebody feel by working with you.

"You will become extremely well organized, which significantly increases your productivity and substantially reduces your stress."

There's multiple emotional connect terms in that pitch.

I could say, "I help people create and grow businesses" because that's what I do, but there is no emotional connection there. You must think about how you make your clients feel by working with you, not just what it is you are selling.

Ask three of your most successful former clients, "How did you feel by working with me?"

Ask your most successful former client, "Why did you hire me?"

Use what your former clients said, to obtain your future clients.

One of my former clients sells art. He is not going to say, "I sell art that's really cool!" He's going to talk about how people feel by purchasing his art.

How do you make people feel when they work with you?

This makes all the difference in the world.

What about when you are talking about your products and services?

It's hard enough for some people to make that emotional connection and when you talk about your products and services, you have to show the value of what you bring.

When you are pitching, there are two elephants.

How do you eat an elephant?

One bite at a time.

The first elephant is creating your pitch, so you can memorize your pitch, and then you can perform your pitch.

When we get to workshop five in negotiations and closing deals, the second elephant is the ability to incorporate their specific needs and make their needs interwoven with your presentation.

You want to have a really clear, concise, well-organized pitch, and here's how you do that.

You say you have three packages: packages A, B, and C.

- Package A has five added values.
- Package B has five added values.
- Package C has five added values.

Then, you want to take the potential client and put them in the shoes of somebody who's already hired you.

You're going to say, "when you hire me" and then state the logistics.

What does it look like when they work with you?

"When you hire me, you work with me for up to one hour per week, you get access to my online program, you get access to my online community. I'm available 24/7 if you need to talk. You'll have one hour of homework, and an entertaining, educational video, you're going to take copious handwritten notes. Ensure that you're not multitasking, so that it pounds in your subconscious."

Tell people exactly what it looks like to work with you before they work with you.

It's the five added values and then the logistics. Since this is an elephant and you are eating it one bite at a time, you don't want to overwhelm yourself by trying to do the whole thing at once.

Slow down.

Do this, step-by-step. Don't try to do it all at once; do it one step at a time, line by line.

Slow down.

This is where everybody goes wrong when they're trying to do this on their own.

Just say Package A and say the first added value of Package A.

Just do that all by itself. Don't think of the big picture. Just do the parts and it will all add up at the end.

Package A: value added number two.

Write that down. Do that right now.

Package A: value added number three.

Just go line by line like that.

At the end of the day, you're going to have the five added values of package A, five added values of package B, five added values of package C, and you're going to have the logistics of each package.

After you say the five added values of package A, you're going to say the logistics, "When you hire me" or "When you work with me" or "When you buy my art."

What is it going to look like for the client?

For example, if you're providing services, which most of my clients do, you're going to send them a survey initially to get input on where they're at right now and where they're looking to go.

You're going to do some research on their product or service or their brand, contingent upon the type of business.

Then you're going to set up a one-hour consultation with them to review what you have figured out so far and figure out the plan moving forward.

Many people use the word I in their pitch.

You have to shift from "I" to "you" because they need to have that feeling of already working with you.

"When you hire me…"

"When you're working with me…"

"This is what's going to happen…"

"By becoming extremely well organized, YOU will…."

Make it forward-facing; make your pitch about them. You will XYZ.

Don't say I or I help. That's horrible.

It's not about you. Your stupid feelings don't matter. Feelings are stupid.

It's about putting them in the shoes of somebody who's already purchased your product or service and showing them what it's going to look like, and you want to say "When you hire me," because it's planting the seed that they're going to hire you.

People will say to me during pitch meetings, "Wait, I'm not interested. I wasn't going to hire you."

I say, "Oh, yeah, no problem!" Even if you're not going to hire me, you need to know what I do, otherwise! You can't refer me.

Anyway, say "When you hire me" and go right back into the "When you hire me" language.

This also shows a clear delineation between the added values and logistics. You don't want to confuse those two things.

This puts people in a definitive position of them thinking about working with you.

That's a huge piece that people miss as we get to talking about your thirty-second pitch, which is what we're moving to next.

I hear so many people say, "I help blah blah blah…"

That's about you, not about them. Everything should be about them.

DO NOT SAY, "I HELP."

Yes, I'm yelling at you again....

The same thing with your about section on your LinkedIn profile.

It should not be your resume. Nothing you say or write should be about you.

It's about what you do for others because the only thing people care about, especially when they're paying you money, is themselves and how they're going to benefit from what you provide.

It has nothing to do with the "why" statement. It is not, "I do what I do because I'm passionate about helping children" or something like that.

Even though it's good to understand your personal why behind your business, it's still not the why.

The why is the reasons why they should hire you and how it will benefit them, not how it will benefit you!

Next step is your thirty-second pitch.

Let's walk through how you can start doing that now.

It's three easy steps:

- your emotional connect line,
- an overview of your packages, and
- one specific call to action.
    1. Emotional connect line
    2. You're not going to call them Package A, B, and C, you're going to say, "You can benefit from...XYZ."
    3. You will name what the packages are and then the call to action such as:
        a. *Please hop on my calendar for a thirty-minute complimentary conversation.*
        b. *"Cause and Effect Consulting is changing the world!"*

"By becoming extremely well organized, you will significantly increase your productivity and substantially reduce your stress. I'm going run you through a six-week business development boot camp, I'm going to beat you with a big ass stick, ignore your stupid feelings, you're going hate me for six weeks, and you'll be in love with me in four months from now."

"Follow me and click the event link in the description to learn more."

I WILL BEAT YOU WITH A BIG ASS STICK. YOU WILL HATE ME FOR 6 WEEKS AND BE IN LOVE WITH ME IN FOUR MONTHS FROM NOW. AFTER THAT, WE MIGHT BE FRIENDS.

Your emotional connect line, an overview of what it is you are selling, whether it is a product or service, and then one call to action.

Don't say free! Don't say "free" meetings… because nobody values free!

Again, people make decisions in the subconscious, based on emotion, not based on logic. You want to say "complimentary." If there's "free" on your website or your LinkedIn, or anywhere else, get rid of it.

Change it to complimentary, because complimentary means value without charge.

We will come back to the two to four-minute pitch after we talk about the eight-minute pitch. There's a couple of different ways you can do the two to four-minute pitches.

The two to four-minute pitches are for when you're at a networking event and you go into a breakout room, you usually get two to four minutes to talk there. Let's get the eight-minute pitch now.

The eight-minute pitch is for when you're actually doing a thirty-minute one-on-one business meeting with somebody.

Your eight-minute pitch is your emotional connect line, then the overview of your three packages, the names, just like a thirty-second pitch, with the five added values and the logistics, but no call to action.

During the eight-minute pitch, you are going to say Package A is this, it has these five added values, and here's what it looks like if you hired me for that one.

Then, you're going to go to Package B, these are the five added values. Here's what it looks like when you hire me for that and tell the logistics there.

Then, package C, those five added values, and then the logistics of what it's going look like when they hire you for that.

Your eight-minute pitch might be five minutes or it might be eight and a half minutes. That exact specific time is not as important as following this particular structure.

When you're actually pitching people, you're going to end up using what they say to you in your pitch to incorporate and make their needs interwoven way.

INCORPORATE THEIR SPECIFIC NEEDS IN AN INTERWOVEN WAY.

You are providing the solutions to their problems which is going to extend the amount of time that your pitch takes. So, that's your eight-minute pitch.

Your two to four-minute pitch can be an abbreviated version of your eight-minute in two different ways.

If you're at a particular networking event and you think one of your three products or services would sell better there, you will just say your emotional connect, the five added values, and the five logistics of that particular package with the call to action.

Or you can just do a brief version of the eight-minute pitch. It's up to you what you want to do there. You've just got less time, so talk about whatever you think is going to land better depending on who you are talking to and where you are at.

With the eight-minute pitch, who talks first?

Always get them to talk first. Whoever talks first loses.

This is how you run a 30-minute business meeting:

1. You're going to research people for thirty minutes to an hour the day before you meet with people.

2. The first minute is: form rapport. Say you found something interesting about them, where they lived, or hobby they have.

A gentleman I know worked in the prison system for five years, so I asked him what that was all about. He said, "That's what I did when I got to college to get my credits to become a counselor." He's said, "you just took me back 25 years."

You are showing the person that you are meeting with that you've invested time into them, which shows that you value them, because you've already researched and studied them.

3. That's one minute, the next two minutes are adding value.

You want to say, "Hey, is it cool if I give you some tips? I researched your website and your LinkedIn profile. Is it okay with you if I give you some input?"

100% of people will say yes.

You don't want to give unsolicited advice.

You want to ask permission to do that. Otherwise, you're going to get a negative reaction if you just start giving advice without permission.

You don't want that kind of energy at the beginning of your business meeting.

"I researched you. Is it cool if I provided you with some feedback?"

That lets them know that you've already invested into them.

Then you can say, "I know you are a financial planner. Your last LinkedIn recommendation is two years old. That's probably really important for your business.

That's a real quick, easy fix: ask for three recommendations and get them to show up on your LinkedIn profile. If you can get three of those, that would help out your brand a lot.

There's no emotional connection at the top of your website and you only have seven seconds to catch somebody's attention when they look at your website or your LinkedIn profile."

Say whatever value you want to add. Just provide massive value within two minutes. Your three top tips for them, based upon your RESEARCH.

TO ADD MASSIVE VALUE MEANS TO SAY SHIT SO IMPORTANT THAT THEY WRITE IT DOWN.

The next thing you will say is, "Please tell me about what you do in your business."

Get them to pitch for eight minutes.

This may be like pulling teeth; most people haven't bought this manual yet; most people have zero idea how to clearly and concisely articulate massive value for their product or service (to pitch).

If they give you some twenty-second bullshit, ask for more. "Please tell me everything you do for your clients."

Take little handwritten notes while they're talking, based upon how you can assist, so that when you're pitching, you can incorporate what they said into your pitch.

Then the last eight minutes of your business meeting, that's the close.

Don't try doing everything all at once. Do this very slowly piece by piece and step by step.

Your Pitch: Let's Get it Done, NOW.

Time to complete your pitch!

To pitch means to clearly and concisely articulate massive value.

Complete this activity before moving forward.

Do this one step at a time; **go super fucking slow**. One thought at a time.

First, list the five added values of each package, then the logistics.

Take the potential client and put them in the shoes of somebody who has already hired you.

Step 1: Create an emotional connection in your pitch. How does your offer help clients to feel better after they hire you? State the why, not the what and the how.

Step 2: What are your products or services?

What is the specific value that your clients will obtain by buying your product or service?

Package 1 Values

- First value you provide:
- Second value you provide:
- Third value you provide:
- Fourth value you provide:
- Fifth value you provide:

Package 2 Values

- First value you provide:
- Second value you provide:
- Third value you provide:
- Fourth value you provide:

- Fifth value you provide:

Package 3 Values

- First value you provide:
- Second value you provide:
- Third value you provide:
- Fourth value you provide:
- Fifth value you provide:

Step 3: What are the logistical steps? What does it look like when I hire you?

Avoid ambiguity; be specific.

Put the potential client in the shoes of somebody who has already hired you.

Package 1 Logistics

- Step 1:
- Step 2:
- Step 3:
- Step 4:
- Step 5:

Package 2 Logistics

- Step 1:
- Step 2:
- Step 3:
- Step 4:
- Step 5:

Package 3 Logistics

- Step 1:
- Step 2:
- Step 3:
- Step 4:
- Step 5:

Your 30-Second Pitch

1. The Emotional Connect
2. State your three package titles:
   - Package 1 Title:
   - Package 2 Title:

- Package 3 Title:
3. Call To Action (CTA): Please schedule a complimentary 30-minute conversation on my calendar!

Your 2 - 4 Minute Pitch:

1. The Emotional Connect
2. Overview of Packages/Logistics:
   - Package 1:
   - Package 2:
   - Package 3:
3. Call To Action (CTA): Schedule a complimentary conversation on my calendar!

The 8-Minute Pitch

1. The Emotional Connect
2. State added values and logistics for each package
   - Package 1 - Values (and then Logistics)
   - Package 2 - Values (and then Logistics)
   - Package 3 - Values (and then Logistics)

There is no CTA on the 8-Minute Pitch because you're already in a 1-on-1 conversation.

CHAPTER TWO:
RETURN ON INVESTMENT (ROI) & CUSTOMER ACQUISITION COST (CAC)

ACTIVITY DOES NOT EQUAL PRODUCTIVITY.

It's time to discuss activity versus productivity.

Activity does NOT equal productivity.

You should not be ripping and running.

You want to look back at the past week, the last three months, six months, nine months, and the past year.

What have you been doing with all your time and money?

Look through your calendar.

Do a deep dive into your bank accounts and credit cards.

What have you really gotten back for all of your effort?

When my clients start working with me, they are always busy, stressed out, overwhelmed, and not productive.

Understanding that being busy is not productive is key.

Being busy is stupid.

There's no wish, hope, luck, or try.

There's no luck in business.

Being busy means you're ripping and running.

The hamster in the wheel is very busy going nowhere.

What is the first step?

The first thing to know and understand is return on investment (ROI).

How much money are you actually making?

Say you get $2,000 on a deal, and then you spent $1,500 to get that deal.

You need to calculate your time too and put a rate on that, so you're not working for yourself for free and you're calculating that into the cost.

If you invest $1,500 and you make $2000, take the two grand minus the amount that it cost you to get that deal, you actually made $500 bucks on that deal.

I had a client who had a speaking engagement that she was very excited about.

I said, "How much are you worth per hour?" She said, "$350 an hour."

Now, I said, "Okay. How many hours are you speaking?

She said, "Two hours," and I said, "How much are they paying?" She said, "$300."

I said, "How much prep time is there?" She said, "One hour and probably one-hour follow-up."

So, it's not $300 for one hour, or $300 for two hours. It's $300 divided by four hours…you're really making $75 bucks an hour.

It's calculating specifically how much time and money you're putting into what you're doing.

- *Are you doing podcasts?*
- *How many clients do you have?*
- *Are you doing networking events?*
- *Are you doing presentations?*
- *Are you doing social media posting marketing? How many? How often? On how many platforms?*
- *What are all the things you've been doing?*
- *And if you've been making money, where has that money been coming from?*

How do you track all of that?

Your activity has to be tracked so you can figure out where you're spending all of your time and your money.

Here is a sample of a document from one of my former clients, which has evolved, as my clients evolve when going through my program.

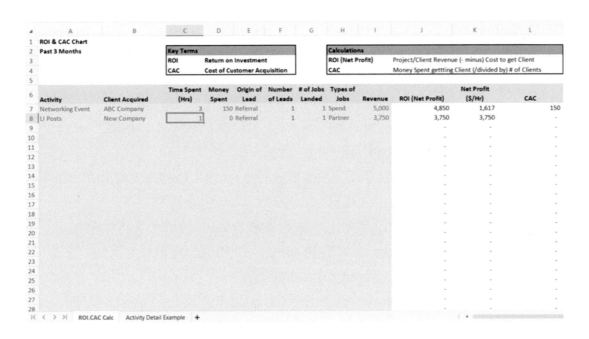

I learn so much by teaching my clients. I have learned from every one of my clients, so my program keeps getting better and better and better.

The document for ROI/CAC, activity versus productivity, will outline everything you need to have prepared. It's a really simple form. It's nothing complicated or overwhelming.

What is the next step after figuring out how to be productive, where your money is going, or how much money you are actually making?

The other major thing you need to calculate is customer acquisition cost (CAC).

If you got two clients, and you spent $200 to get them, you divide the amount of money you spent to get your clients by the number of clients required.

So, for two clients you spent $200. $200 divided by two is $100. That means you spent $100 to acquire each client.

Knowing how much time and money you're spending on everything is really important.

If you say, "I made $1,000!" but you spent ten hours on it and you invested $500 bucks, you did not make $1,000.

You have to take the $500 out of the $1000 you made which now you're at $500, divided by the 10 hours you put into it, you are actually making $50 bucks an hour.

It's really important to see how much money you are actually making.

Most people find out that they need to significantly increase their prices, especially women. It's about charging market value.

If you don't know what you should be charging, at least in my experience, it has been predominantly women who don't charge enough money, research the market value. Men do this too. You probably need to substantially increase your rates.

You have to research the market value for what you provide.

When my clients do this, their minds get blown. A lot of times, you are charging three to five thousand dollars: $3000 for one package and $5000 for one for another package.

One of my clients quadrupled her revenue within six months, because she raised her rates, and now she's charging what she's worth.

Everybody's going to hustle you out of money.

One of my former clients met with Amazon and they said they didn't pay rates like that.

Another one of my former clients met with Disney and they said they "didn't pay rates like that."

All it is, is that they've got better lawyers, better sales reps, and better negotiators.

We're talking about some of the companies that have the most wealth in the world.

When you negotiate with them, they obviously tell you they don't have any money. It is standing up for what you're actually worth and the value you provide.

You can't be desperate for money, or you will end up being desperate. Be the pimp, not the whore. Stand up for your worth.

You have to be able to walk away from the deal.

One of my former clients had a deal pending: ten workshops with Amazon. She told them her rates, and that her rate was her rate.

They said, "We don't pay that."

She said, "No problem."

Three weeks later, Amazon got in touch with her and hired her, at her stated rate.

Having that confidence in your value and your offer when you're discussing your rates is essential.

If you don't have the confidence to ask for the money, think about what you are worth in dollars: all of your experience, your education, and all of the value you bring.

You don't want to end up making $5 an hour or $20 an hour. You can probably go work at a burger joint right now for $20 an hour.

It doesn't make sense as an entrepreneur to have a rate that's not worth what your market value is.

I wouldn't work with my clients, if I didn't think they weren't worth a lot of money.

I had a potential client who wanted to do business bookkeeping.

He asked, "Do you think I can be successful at this for small and medium businesses?"

I said, "Yes. I rarely see anybody telling people, at networking events, that this is a service they provide."

He had 17 years' experience in his area of expertise, and I asked him how much money he wanted to make extra per year because he wanted to keep his job so he could keep his benefits.

He said "$50,000 a year." That's easy, right? One client at four grand a month, and you're at $48,000. So, it's not really hard to hit $50,000 per year.

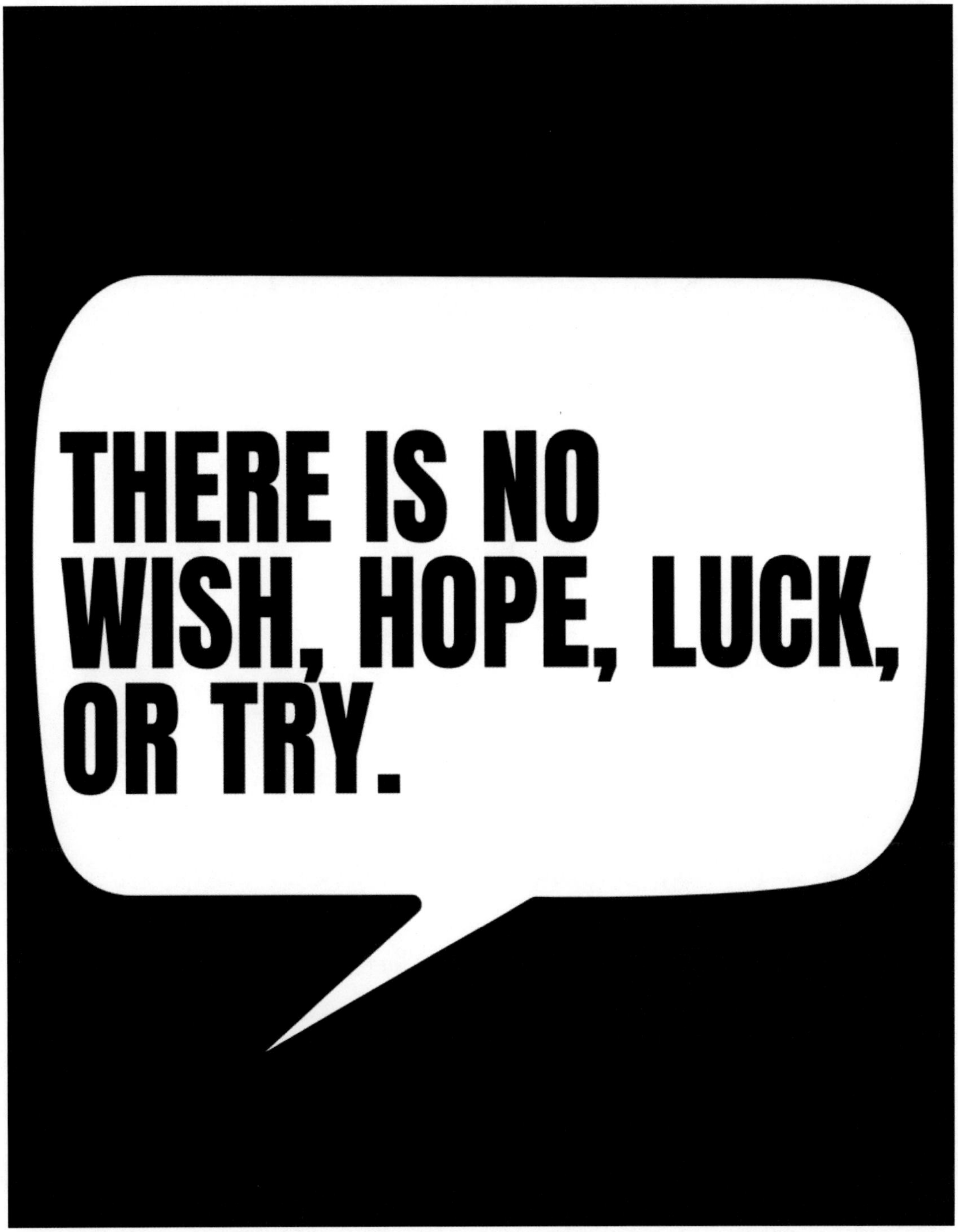
THERE IS NO
WISH, HOPE, LUCK,
OR TRY.

You have got to believe in your value.

It's not your value based on your self-esteem or your self-worth.

It's the market value of the service you provide.

A great way to think about this is: what is the value to the person?

- How much money are they making if you teach them:
- *How to close 90% more deals?*
- *How to be more confident in public speaking?*
- *You teach someone how to market themselves?*
- *How to run their social media efficiently and effectively?*
- *How much is their return on investment for the value you are providing?*

Return On Investment (ROI) & Customer Acquisition Cost (CAC)

    1. Activity does not equal productivity.

    2. What are you doing with your time? *(e.g. presentations, podcasts, networking, social media, etc.)*

    3. What are you doing with your money? *(e.g. ads, memberships, your social media expert, coaches, etc.)*

    4. What are you getting in return?

ROI

The amount of money brought in by project/client:

- Minus - The amount that it cost (in accurate terms):

You can then divide the gross by the hours you put into it. How much did you get paid per hour? Don't short yourself.

Be your own BOSS. Be honest with yourself.

CAC

The amount of money spent getting clients:

- Divided By –

The number of clients acquired:

Answer these questions:

- Where are you spending all your time?
- Where are you spending all your money?
- What is that actually getting back?
- Why are you doing the things you are doing?
- What's working and what's not?

Look back at your last three months, six months, nine months, and year.

Your stupid fucking feelings do not matter.

How much money are you making? From where? How? Why?

CHAPTER THREE: MAPPING

IF IT DOESN'T PAY ALL OF YOUR BILLS, YOU DON'T HAVE A BUSINESS, YOU HAVE A HOBBY.

What is Mapping and how do you do it?

Do you have a set clear financial goal?

An exact and specific number?

Do you have a strategy to get there?

A dream without a plan is a wish.

If it doesn't pay all of your bills, you don't have a business, you have a hobby.

Mapping is creating your action plan and strategy for your specific, quantifiable financial goal.

The first thing you want to know is to look at your personal nut and your professional nut.

Know your exact break even. If you have a spouse, it usually works best if you do this with your spouse. So, every $5 you're spending.

On the personal side, even my client who was a CFO for 17 years was forgetting stuff.

You need to include food, vacation, Sirius XM, YouTube, and every subscription and account you have to know exactly how much money you need to break even personally.

On the professional side: insurance, accountants, attorneys, taxes, and software programs.

Make sure that you've added up all your numbers so that you know your exact break even and be as specific as possible. Even if you think you got your stuff in line, you're probably forgetting something.

Take into account getting your hair, nails, and lashes done. It is very eye-opening because those things are all an expense.

Before one of my former clients went through his numbers, he thought his break even was $3,000 a month and it was $11,000 a month and he goes, "Oh, this is why I'm broke all of the time!"

This happened to me as well.

When I had my tech company, my brother and I were pulling out $2,000 a month each. And before I went in and dug deep into all my numbers. I thought my bills were less than $2,000. So, after a year, my brother had around $15,000 in the bank, and I had $8,000 in credit card debt.

The company was making enough money that I could have pulled out more and I knew my brother wasn't a scam artist but then I was confused; "how do you have $15k and I have negative eight?"

It's because my bills were more than $2,000. His bills were $1,500. He didn't drive a car. He didn't go out with girls. He had an apartment with a roommate. That was half the rent, half the utilities, etc.

Know your exact numbers, because you can create the plan to make this a successful business or an even more successful business.

Life is a lot more expensive than you think it is.

You don't know exactly, personally and professionally, what you are spending in the first place.

If you're saying, "Well, on the business side, I don't have insurance, attorneys, accountants, business development, or pay for marketing."

You want to budget for that because you're going to have all of those costs.

You're paying for email, Zoom, Otter, your CRM, your online course to be hosted, website hosting, etc.

All of the little things. I'm sure everybody can relate to this, everybody is charging you $5 for something. The little things matter.

Even for email now, they want $5 a month so your emails don't get deleted. You want to add up all of those things, so you know your exact break even.

Look at the cost of networking groups: some are not cheap, some don't cost any money, some are expensive; factor in all of those things.

Knowing your exact break even might be one of the biggest aha moments in your business. Know your personal and your business numbers.

ROI/CAC activity vs. productivity leads into the mapping. The strategy comes from the research.

For an event, you could be spending $100 here and $100 there. One of the events made you $10,000, the other one made you $500, and **it was the same amount of time, same amount of money investment.**

One of them made you $500 and one of them made you $10,000.

This happens with many of my clients, even my clients who are multi-millionaires and own multiple companies. One of them said, "Wait. That business is making me all that money and the other one is making me no money?"

The numbers don't lie, they tell you what's going on. The business where he put most of his time and effort was the business that made him the least amount of money. The business that he put the least amount of effort into was the one that made him the most amount of money.

Whether it's multiple businesses or multiple ways in which you're attempting to generate your revenue, knowing exactly where that's coming from, knowing exactly what the break even is, personally and professionally, and knowing where you're investing your time and money.

Then, you can move on to the next step, which is creating your strategy.

The numbers don't lie. The little things matter. Every little thing matters.

What's next?

You want to have a bigger goal. You want a specific quantifiable goal.

You don't want to say, "I want my business to do better."

That's not measurable.

It's not quantifiable.

You want a specific number, and no numbers are irrational or unreasonable.

A dream without a plan is a wish.

It can be $300,000 a year. It could be $500,000 a year. No number is irrational or unreasonable, but a dream without a plan is a wish.

It can be any number you want, but you have got to plan out how you're going to get there.

One of my clients had a goal of making $10 million in the next three years. He had three businesses, and I looked at one of his businesses, and he was making $44.64 per hour off of that business.

He would have to work 609 hours per day to get to his goal.

Nothing is irrational or unrealistic.

A dream without a plan is a wish, so it has to be a rational plan.

You are going to take your bigger goal, say $300,000 a year and then you're going to break it down into five smaller goals to get to that point.

You need action steps with due dates and milestones. Your milestones need quantifiable measurements.

For example, I'm sponsoring a golf course right now. I had to pay the guy that owned the golf course. I had to have my writer write something. She gave that to my marketing guy. He edited it. They gave it to my graphic designer who added the QR code and the logo.

The goal was to sponsor a golf course.

The action steps are all of the things I just named. Each one gets a due date. Everybody on my team for that project knew when they needed to get their part done. Each part was contingent upon the other parts.

You want to have that in order and then the quantifiable measurement for ROI is at least five clients within two months because sponsoring a golf course is expensive.

Put whatever you want into your plan when you are mapping out your strategy.

You are doing podcasts, presentations, social media posts, and networking groups. Do these different activities, measure them out, and you want to stay consistent with what you do.

Don't keep hopping around to different networking groups. Stay in the same ones. Do the same thing for 90 days.

Even if you're saying in your head right now, I already did this shit, and it didn't work. It's because you didn't know how to show value before.

DON'T THINK. JUST DO EXACTLY WHAT I SAY!

From chapter one, you now know how to show value.

From chapter two, you kind of know what was working and it might not have been working, because you didn't know how to show value before.

Don't abandon everything you've been doing.

If you know for sure it's crap, stop doing it, but everything is not crap. If everything has been crap, that's because it's your fault.

You are not doing a good job of showing value.

Do what you do for 90 days and calculate it.

Spend one hour a week taking a look back at the past week and seeing where the people you are meeting with are coming from.

- *Where did the people on your calendar come from?*
- *What networking events got people on your calendar?*
- *What networking events or activities produce the meetings with qualified leads?*

A qualified lead is somebody with money and the desire for your services.

Figure out where those people go and go there.

In 2022, 70% of my clients were coming from LinkedIn posts.

Now, most of my clients come from referrals.

You might get a referral from a former client or from doing a presentation.

Make sure you put a lot of effort into presenting and maintaining the relationships with your former clients.

You will create your own strategy broken down into small parts with action steps, due dates, and milestones.

After you have your goals, milestones, and action steps…what do you do next?

Start doing these things. Don't sit there and keep analyzing.

Always operate with intention but don't be concerned with the outcome.

If you're going to go to a networking event for an hour, you should get at least two one-on-one meetings scheduled afterward.

If you're saying "Well, I don't know how many people I am going to meet with."

That is the problem. You are the problem. You are your own problem.

DM at least three people per hour and say:

"I'd love to hear more about what you do and tell you about what I do! Here's my calendar, if you want to talk: XXXXXXXXXXXX"

This shit is easy.

Don't make it complicated.

Don't concern yourself with how many people DON'T respond.

"The how is none of your business." ~Les Brown

Just put in the work.

Stop hiding and expecting money to just come to you.

Take yourself outside of yourself and look at yourself and be honest.

You need to tell yourself what to do, like you are your own boss because you are your own boss in entrepreneurship.

If you were your employee, would you promote or fire you?

Be honest....

Are you holding yourself strictly accountable?

If you had a job, you wouldn't be able to do whatever WHENEVER.

That's what you're doing right now.

You're fucking around, a lot.

Fucking focus.

Tell yourself how many people you're going to meet with.

How do you do that?

What you do is, after the networking event, find somebody that you think what they talked about was interesting.

Message them directly and say, "Hey, Michelle! What you spoke about today was really interesting. I'd love to hear more about what you do and tell you about what I do."

Now, you want to be clear when you're messaging people, so you say, "I want to hear about what you do AND tell you about what I do."

You want to be clear about what your intention is.

Because when you meet with them, if you had just said, "I'd love to hear more about what you do."

They will feel like you did a bait and switch on them and that you were really there just to sell them.

Be honest about your intention with what you do. You want to be pitching everybody you meet with.

If you don't tell people what you do, they can't hire you and they can't refer you.

In every meeting, you should be letting people know what you do, even if it's not a qualified lead.

TAKE YOURSELF OUTSIDE OF YOURSELF AND LOOK AT YOURSELF.

There's three thoughts to have going into an eight-minute pitch meeting.

This is the "operate with intention and don't be concerned with the outcome" broken down into a greater nuance.

Three major thoughts headed into every business meeting:

- *Number one: Everybody has money.*
- *Number two: Everybody needs my help.*
- *Number three: This person is going to hire me.*

Confucius said, "He who thinks he can, and he who thinks he cannot are both correct."

"Most people had already lost in the locker room." Mike Tyson

What is your self-talk?

Do not make the decision for the potential buyer.

If they don't want to buy, that's fine, but don't disqualify them. Let them decide if they want what you have or not.

You're talking yourself out of a lot of fucking money.

EVERYBODY HAS MONEY. EVERYBODY NEEDS MY HELP. THIS PERSON IS GOING TO HIRE ME.

Many times, my clients go into meetings thinking, "Oh, this person doesn't have money." Or, "This person doesn't need me."

They've researched them the night before….

You've screwed up your energy.

You've already lost the fight before you even got into the ring.

You've already predetermined the loss.

You've decided you're going to lose before you go in.

You want to operate with intention and don't be concerned with the outcome.

Don't get upset if people don't hire you.

Because then you'll have negative energy, which might cost you on your next deal. Think positive thoughts going into your meeting!

You also can't make someone's decision for them. You don't know where they are. You don't know if they have money or if they don't have money.

People have money for the things they want.

People that are impoverished near me, on the West Side of Chicago, have $300 shoes and they have $1,000 cell phones.

People always find the money for all the things that they want.

People drink, smoke, go out to eat, go on vacations…People waste money on all kinds of stuff.

People have money.

Are you showing massive value? Are you incorporating their specific needs, in an interwoven manner?

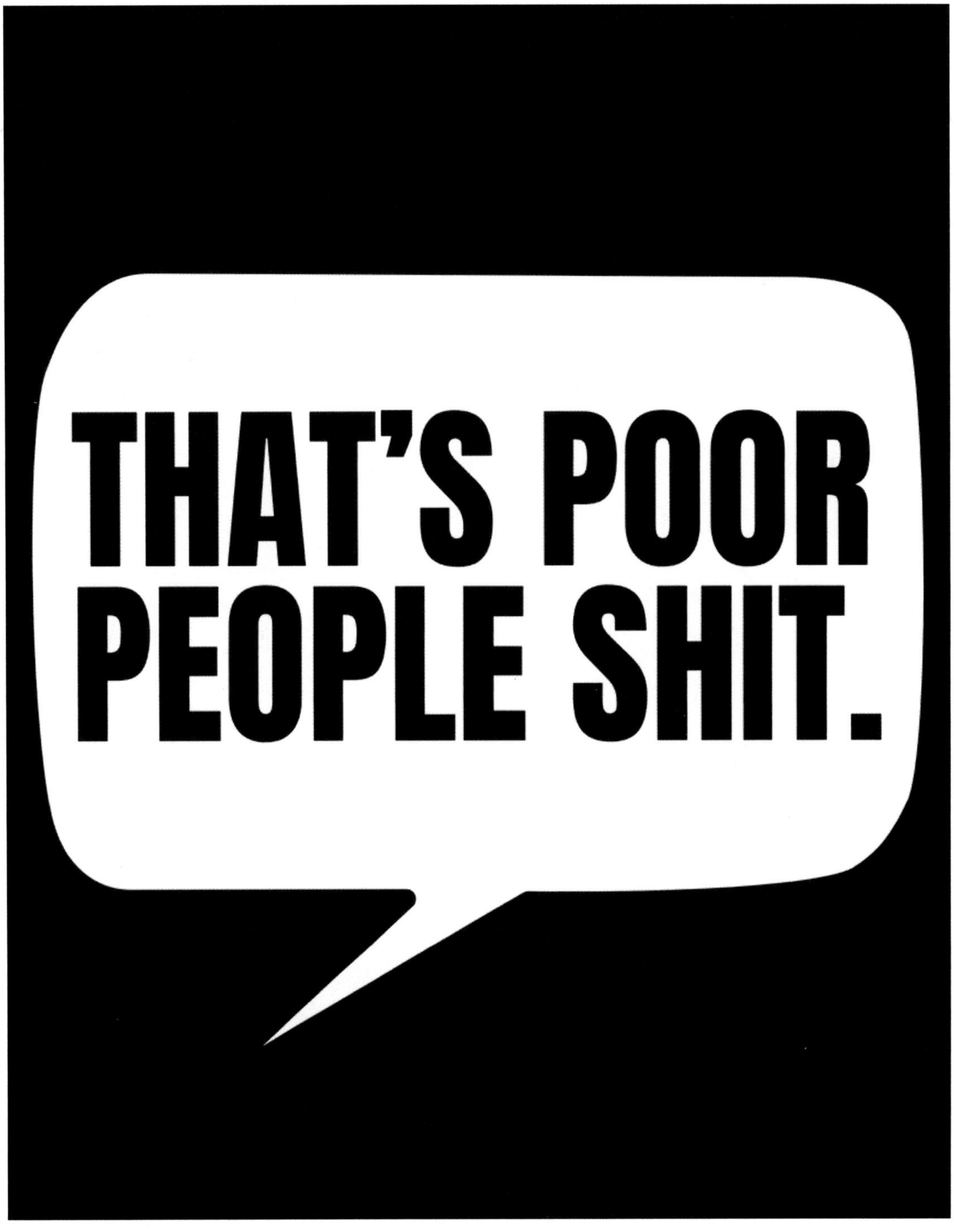
THAT'S POOR PEOPLE SHIT.

It's about whether or not you are showing enough value for them to believe that it's worth their money.

Don't ever have a pitch meeting and then say, "They didn't have money, or they didn't see the value in what I do."

Always blame yourself for everything.

It's the only way to grow.

If they said they didn't have money, that's because they didn't think their money was worth spending on you, because you didn't show enough value.

This means you didn't do a good job of incorporating enough value for them specifically.

Always look at yourself with everything. It's the only thing you can control.

Make sure that you print out your mapping sheet and put it everywhere so you can see it.

One of my clients made it her screensaver so she was looking at it all the time. Print it out. Put it where you go a lot: on your refrigerator, in your bathroom.

This is a living document. This is what should be guiding your activities.

Don't change it until after 90 days. **Stay consistent** with what you do for 90 days. Don't jump all over the place.

**Don't chase the shiny objects, stay consistent.

If nothing comes of it, if you have these five activities you're doing, get rid of the two that are doing nothing. Keep the three that are generating leads or revenue or both.

Don't just jump all over the place.

People need to see you consistently on LinkedIn, on different social media platforms, at networking events, and doing presentations.

They need to see you over and over again. There's a lot of different rules people say, the rule of 12 touches. If you are going to multiple events. Over time people have developed a relationship with you because they keep seeing you over and over again and you're consistent.

Consistency is key and with a mapping, so some people may over analyze. STOP THINKING. Take massive action and stay consistent. It will work.

How do you break free of that?

You are going to get the documentation that you need to do this.

Everything is KISS: Keep It Simple Stupid. Or Keep It Stupid Simple

At the end of this manual, you will be very happy and say all this stuff was really simple.

It's taking difficult concepts and ones that are extremely impactful on whether somebody's successful or not and making them really simple.

Create a simple document like the example you've been given and don't overthink it. Don't over complicate it.

Podcasts: two a week

Presentations: two a week

Networking events: five a week

State specifically which ones you are going to be doing.

Your Map

Step 1: What is your exact break-even or "Nut"?

Exact Personal Budget: $$$$$$

Exact Professional Budget: $$$$$$

Step 2: What is your Overall Goal?

State a specific financial number.

How much do you want to make above your Nut?

Step 3: What are your ROI and CAC?

How much do you make (on average) per client?

How many qualified leads do you have to speak to land one?

Step 4: Create Action Steps with Due Dates and Milestones.

Five Smaller Goals:

> 1. Small Goal 1:
> 2. Small Goal 2:
> 3. Small Goal 3
> 4. Small Goal 4:
> 5. Small Goal 5:

Action Steps (assign a specific due date to each one):

Milestones (assign a quantifiable measurement, a number, that defines success or failure):

For example, I'm sponsoring a golf course right now.

I had to:

> 1. Pay the owner of the golf course
> 2. Have my copywriter write something.

3. My marketing director edited it and sent it to my graphic designer.

4. He added the QR Code and the logo.

Those are the action steps.

Each one of those gets a due date.

The quantifiable measurement is five clients within two months.

This is a sample of what mapping looks like.

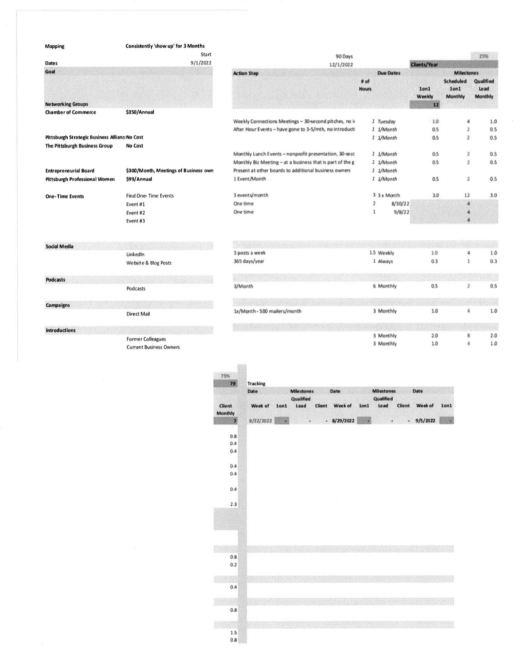

CHAPTER FOUR: LOOSE ENDS: YOUR OPPORTUNITY TO ASK ME A MILLION QUESTIONS WHEN YOU HIRE ME

THAT'S BUSINESS ADVICE!

This is your opportunity to catch up and ask me a million questions when you hire me.

Half of my program is set in stone, half of my program is organic, based on my client's specific needs.

You have now completed scheduling, branding, pitching, packages, and processes, and created a strategy for success.

When you hire me, this is your opportunity to catch up and ask me a million questions.

Please come prepared with questions when you hire me.

Everything in writing

Make sure you get EVERYTHING in writing.

- If things are NOT in writing, people will interpret what you said.
- If stuff was sent via text, screencap EVERYTHING.
- If it was a zoom meeting, record it. Get it transcribed. Send it to the person and have them acknowledge it.

NEVER let them INTERPRET.

At the top of an SOP write:

- **Do NOT interpret.**

At the bottom of an SOP write:

- **Do NOT interpret.**

Ask questions—there are NO stupid questions.

CHAPTER FIVE:
NEGOTIATIONS AND CLOSING DEALS

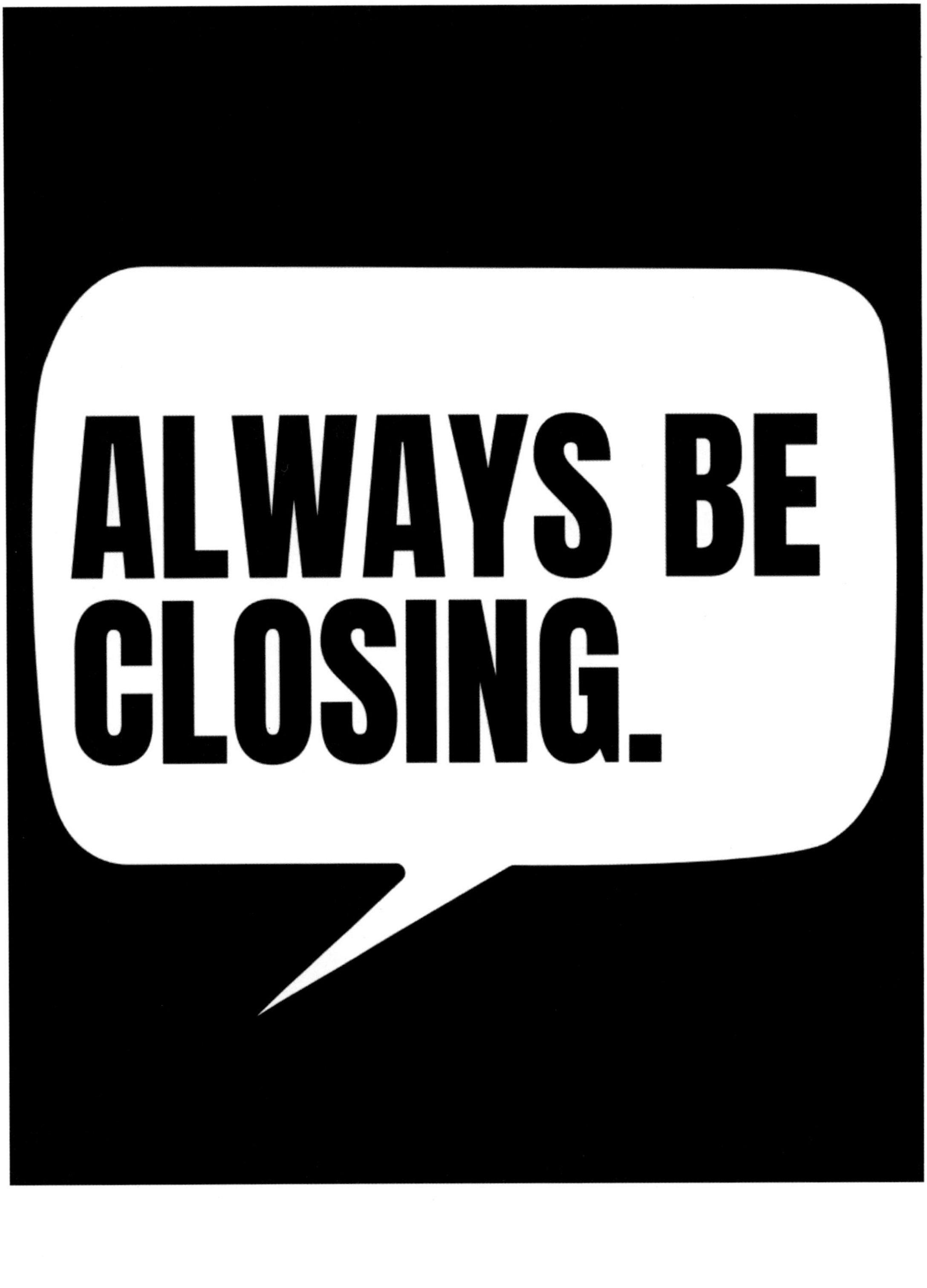
ALWAYS BE CLOSING.

Welcome to chapter five: negotiations and closing deals.

How do you increase your closing rates?

There are many different ways to do that.

Make sure you always start with your emotional connection.

By now, your calendar should be booked out for the next month or two.

Make sure your Calendly calendar has specific questions.

Make sure your calendar questions are specific and intentional.

Your questions may have evolved at this point, so go back and review your calendar questions.

Your questions should NOT be project management questions.

Ask the questions you need to know, and you might want to change them up at this point since you know a lot more now than you did five weeks ago.

One of my former clients owned a social media company and one of my former clients owns a website development company. They were asking project management questions.

You want to ask the emotional connection questions:

1. *What is the current situation for your business?*
2. *What are your barriers?*
3. *What does outrageous success look like for you in six months now?*

Then, you already have all of that data and information going into the meeting.

The meeting breakdown again. Here it is.

ON TIME IS LATE.

Research people for 30 minutes to an hour the day before you meet with people.

The first minute of the meeting is to form rapport.

The next two minutes of the meeting you will add massive value and then get them to talk first.

An intelligent negotiator is going to try to get you to talk first.

Whoever talks first loses.

Be the pimp, not the whore.

It's your meeting; run your meetings.

Write down little handwritten notes, not copious notes, when they are saying their pain points or barriers or their dreams.

Take notes on what solutions you have to their problems.

Then you present for 8 minutes.

You are presenting the same pitch every time and it's customized to that person.

You are incorporating their specific needs, the problems they had, your solutions to those problems, and how you're going to help them accomplish their goals or dreams.

An older person will say they have dreams and a younger person is going say they have goals. Young people don't like the word dreams.

The way to land way more deals is to have way more information going into the meeting.

You have to be in control of the meeting.

A lot of people are brainwashed by know, like, and trust, Go-Giver, and all about relationships. They're going to want to do a "get to know you" meeting.

Do NOT do "get to know you" meetings. **Run business meetings.** Follow the format specifically as laid out.

Before your pitch, how are you finding out what their pain points are?

You are doing that in three different ways.

1. Having them get on your Calendly calendar and asking the correct questions.
2. Researching them.
3. Having them speak first.

You do that in your calendar survey.

You're asking questions on your calendar and you are doing that when you are researching them before you meet with them.

What is their current status?

What are their current barriers?

What does outrageous success look like for them six months from now?

For a guy who does website design and development, it's easy for him.

He is seeing how long it takes for their website to load. He's seeing if they have an emotional connection on their website.

He is seeing what kind of file types they are using on their website, and if it gives the website the best aesthetic appeal or not.

You are asking them the appropriate questions as well.

When you're taking those notes, you're finding out what their pain points are and taking notes, so you can go back to those pain points and solve their problems.

People will try to talk themselves out of closing the deal.

There are several major problems that can occur when you are asking for the sale.

You have to have emotional intelligence too.

When they are ready to buy, you need to shut your stupid mouth and take their fucking money.

You have to shut your mouth and take their money when they say they are ready to buy.

I saw a client do a pitch the other day and the client, the person she was pitching to said, "I need to hire you."

My client continued to sell and talk about value, instead of going into the part where you actually close the deal.

Another one of my clients said, "It's a switch off."

You're switching from the part of adding massive value, which is what you've been doing the whole time, to going into the sales mentality.

Which is actually closing the deal.

You have to ask for the sale.

Don't state the price until they ask for the price.

When they ask for the price, say it in a deep voice, a grown man's voice, "$10,000" and then shut the fuck up.

Don't say anything else after that. Whoever talks first loses.

Don't state the price until they ask for the price, make sure that you state the price confidently, and then be quiet and see what they say.

They're going to bring up two major barriers.

"I don't really have the time for this right now" or "I don't have the money for this right now." If it's a matter of money, that's easy.

Ask, "What can you afford to put down right now? Can you afford half?"

Have them put down half and put it in writing.

It's only a deal when they send you money and confirm the agreement in writing.

Now, you have got to listen really closely.

What I see my clients do is, the person will say, "I can't really afford this right now."

Then they will go back to talking about the value of what they provide.

The person did not say, "I don't see value."

They said, "I don't think I can afford this right now."

Listen really closely to what they say, so you can focus on whatever it is that you're overcoming.

What is the correct barrier to overcome?

Listening is key and a lot of people make that mistake by not listening to what they're saying and going to a completely different subject.

If they're not buying, whose fault is it?

Yours. Always take accountability.

You don't want to submit written proposals with numbers on them.

The number one premise in my program is to always blame yourself for everything so you can grow.

If your written proposal gets rejected, you never know why. You can't follow up or else you look like an idiot.

Nothing is a failure. If you keep feeling like you are failing, you are not. As long as you are learning from it, it is not a failure.

Some people will say, "Well, they didn't appreciate my value."

That means you did a poor job of stating your specific solutions to their specific problems in an interwoven manner.

Don't say, "They didn't have money."

They had money.

As we already discussed, people have money for the things they see value in. If they didn't see value in it, you did a poor job of incorporating their needs and showing that you provided the solutions to their specific needs.

What if they are hesitant about moving forward?

What is preventing them from moving forward?

Is it a good idea to ask them or not?

The person will tell you how to sell them.

They will tell you what they need from you.

They'll tell you why they're not buying.

Is it a good idea to ask them what barriers they are facing?

Take yourself outside of yourself and look at yourself.

You will meet with 12 people per week.

Six thirty-minute meetings on Thursday and six thirty-minute meetings on Friday.

It's forty-eight people per month. You are going to land three to five deals a month.

If you charge five grand, that's $15k to $25k month, and **it's mostly failure.**

You cannot have negative energy.

You cannot have negative energy, because if you get nine doors slammed in your face, that tenth door might be the deal.

You're not going to get that deal if your energy sucks.

You have got to be great every single time and you have got to have fun with it.

You can't be boring, and you can't be desperate. If you have a desperate attitude.

If you're desperate to land a deal, you're going to stay desperate.

A lot of clients say to me, "If I could just land one deal."

You are never going to land that deal. That one deal is never going to happen.

I get a lot of clients because I don't care.

I'm not concerned with the outcome. I operate with intention, and I'm not concerned with the outcome.

You want to hire me? Hire me. You don't, then don't. I don't care.

I'm not going to be desperate for money. That creates a weird energy when you're talking to somebody who desperately wants something from you.

YOU ARE THE PROBLEM....YOU NEED TO TAKE RESPONSIBILITY AND GET OUT OF YOUR OWN WAY.

Let's go into how to run a business meeting again.

Make sure you research people for thirty to sixty minutes the day before you meet with them. It's going to make all the difference in the world.

You will get no calls, no shows. It's okay. You already know a lot about that person.

Never contact them again; do not respond if they contact you again; be the pimp, not the whore.

Maybe that'll be handy later on, or maybe you're learning things through that process.

You're definitely going to lose deals if you haven't invested in the person in advance.

You're not going to be able to articulate massive value if you don't even know who you're dealing with.

Do the research number one.

Number two: the first minute of your meeting form rapport.

Say something interesting about their background, like, "Oh, you played tennis in high school, so did I." Or, "I noticed you traveled around a lot. Were your parents in the military?" Say something that shows you invested time in them.

The next two minutes add massive value. Start with, "May I please offer some input? I researched you and looked at your website. Is it cool if I provide some input on what I saw?"

Never provide unsolicited advice! Everybody hates that! Ask for permission first.

Talk to them about their LinkedIn "About" section.

Is it about other people or does it look like a CV resume?

Is there an emotional connection at the top of their profile or website?

Is it clear what products and services are providing?

Are their recommendations up to date?

Just give them positive, useful value.

You want to add value, you don't want to do sales.

You want to add value to the point where people say, "Man! If this is what I got out of thirty minutes with you, I need to hire you! I can't imagine what would happen in six weeks with you."

One minute: form rapport, two minutes add value. Get them to talk first for eight minutes, and take little handwritten notes. Then, when you pitch, incorporate their specific needs into your pitch. Incorporate their needs and make it interwoven.

I do this…you have this problem…this is what I do to help solve your problem.

During the last eleven minutes, you close the deal.

You are figuring out if they're going to hire you. If they ask the price, they are interested in hiring you.

So then you can close the deal. You have to anticipate the close before it happens.

Before a person has totally decided that they're going to hire me, they are thinking, "I think I am going to do this."

I say, "Alright, cool! I meet with my clients on Mondays for one hour per week. It needs to be consistent for six weeks. Can you take a look at your calendar and let me know what time works for you on Mondays?"

"I can do one o'clock on Mondays."

"Are you sure that's going to work for you for the next six weeks? Check it out."

"Yeah, I can do that."

"Ok great! How do you like to send money?"

Make it as easy as possible to send money.

Do not make it difficult to buy.

Don't tell them, "This is how I take money."

Say, "How do you like to send money?"

Whatever they say, is your favorite way to take money.

That's why you can have CashApp, Zelle, Wise, Venmo, Stripe, and PayPal. PayPal takes too much money. Wise takes nothing.

I'm not going to tell somebody, "this is the only way I take money."

"I can take credit cards with my bank business account too. However you want to pay, I can take your money!"

Don't say you're going to send them an invoice.

When they're ready to buy, I say, "I'm going to put the link in the chat. Can you please click on that link to make sure it works? You know how these things are. A lot of times they don't work."

Anytime somebody leaves a meeting with you and you haven't closed the deal, they're going to say," I need to think it over."

Say, "Okay, that's cool." Ask them, "What is it that you need to think over?"

Because as soon as they leave, they are going to say, "I don't have the time for this right now. I can't really afford this right now. I don't know if you are the right person to work with right now."

It's all negative self-talk because they are scared. You have got to hold their hand. You have to be confident for them, that they're making the right decision.

Think about any time you buy anything.

When I bought a washing machine a while back, I was constantly anxious about making a buying decision.

"Am I buying the right one?"

"Are these people legitimate?"

"Is this the right brand?"

"Oh, I had this other brand and it broke right away."

You know, there's anxiety when you're spending money and when you are making a purchase. You have to be confident for the person. That they are making the right decision.

And take their money. Take the money.

Always take the money.

If your calendar is booked two months out and someone says they want to meet with you now, ask them, "Is it because you want to hire me?" If they say yes, then say, "I can talk to you tonight." If they say no, then say, "Use my calendar link."

By taking that call it gives the person a sense that:

- You are treating them special. Hormone shit.
- It triggers their adrenaline to work with you meaning….
- It creates a **sense of urgency.**
- ON TOP OF an **understanding of scarcity.**

This makes it so much easier to close on the first call.

You ALWAYS want to close on the first call.

You can't be insecure.

You can't be successful as an entrepreneur if you can't do sales.

You can't do sales if you lack confidence.

You have to understand the value you're providing is worth a lot more than the money that you are charging. People in theory always say that, but in practice, they don't believe it.

I know that I am worth a lot more money than I charge based on what my prior clients have said to me.

If you haven't had prior clients before, think about the impact of what you have learned has done for you and what that will do for others. You have to understand that what you're charging is worth way more than what you're charging or you're not going to be able to sell it.

You cannot be insecure during the close.

A client of mine had a lady ask the price and they said "$5000. Is that okay?"

That's bad.

You can not ask if your fucking price is okay!

You have to be good with asking for the sale. You have to be confident with accepting money. Money is just an exchange; there is no barter system anymore.

You have to be comfortable with receiving money. The more comfortable you are with receiving money, the more money is going to come to you.

I would not suggest doing what I'm about to say, but I'll tell you what I do sometimes.

This happened in a business meeting because the lady and I had such great rapport. She even said, "I have a crush on you. I don't mean it like that...but I have a crush on you." I said, "I don't mind if you have a crush on me. I'd appreciate it if you did."

At the end of the conversation, she didn't ask the price.

I said, "So are you going to hire me or what?" I wouldn't suggest this for everyone. It's because we had such good rapport that I could do that. But you know, if they seem interested and they haven't asked the price, I do say, "Yeah. You haven't asked me the price yet." Then it goes on from there.

It's a lot of self-confidence and understanding your self-worth.

Again, it's not your worth. It's the worth and the value of the thing you are providing.

How much of a difference is what you offer making in people's lives?

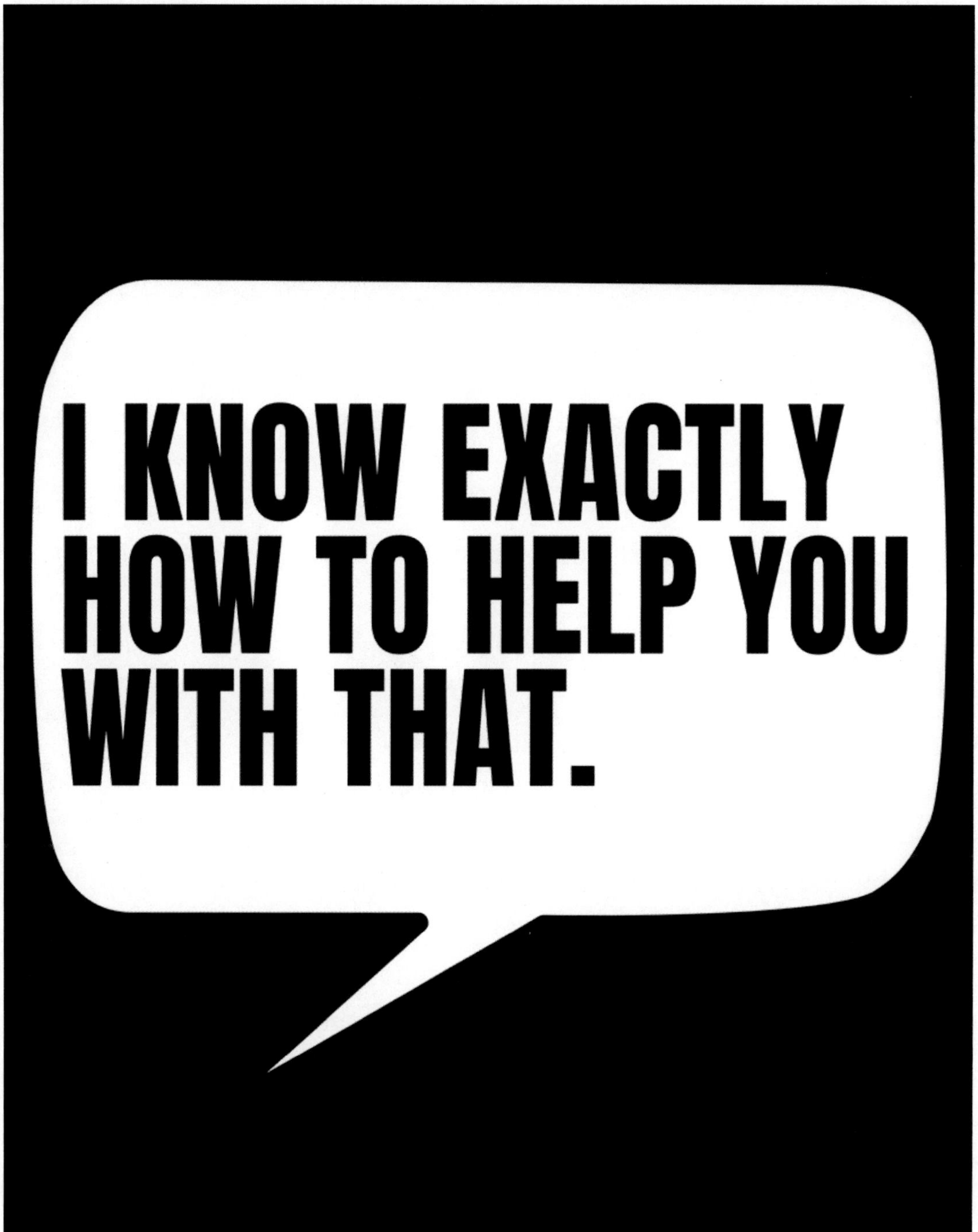
I KNOW EXACTLY HOW TO HELP YOU WITH THAT.

Checklist

Research the person you're meeting with for 30 minutes **the day before** the meeting.

The day of the meeting, spend a few minutes to refresh your recollection of the research before the meeting.

- What value are you showing?
- Why are they meeting with you?
- Do you have a pre-meeting survey that will set the agenda?
- Are you asking the appropriate questions on your calendar survey to close the deal?
  1. What is their current status?
  2. What barriers are they facing?
  3. What does outrageous success look like for them six months from now?
- Are you closing when emotions are high? Close on the first call. At least, plan to close on the first call.
- Are you addressing pain points (specific business problems the person has)?
- Are you addressing their specific pain points in an INTERWOVEN manner with your solutions?
- Are you overcoming barriers (could also be a pain point, or something else, such as price or lack of time?
- Are you asking the right questions during the pitch?
- Are you speaking as if they are going to hire you?
- Are you telling people the process of working with you?
- What are you doing wrong to cause people not to buy?
- Are you interweaving their specific needs into your pitch?
- When you present, are you specifically stating solutions to their specific problems?
- Are you blaming yourself for everything so you can improve?
- Record your pitch meetings. Go back and watch them. Are you following the business meeting structure laid out in this manual?
- Are you being hyper self-critical, without taking it personally?

Do not say to yourself, I did this and this and this correctly, and I could have done this better. Only focus on and look for how to improve your performance.

Supporting Documents
How To Increase Your Close Rate

- Always take yes for an answer; don't talk yourself out of deals.

- Never discuss prices, always discuss value.

- If they're not buying, you're doing a poor job of showing value; always blame yourself for everything; that's the only way to improve.

- Never submit written proposals; you won't get to see their face to know when they find something objectionable.

If they request a written proposal, first ask, "Is there a question that I didn't answer?" If that doesn't work, then say, "I'll write something up, and we can set up a time to talk again, to ensure that we have a meeting of the minds." Do not submit written proposals with numbers on them!!!!

- When they say, "How much does that cost?" That means they're ready to buy, close the deal.

- State the price in a deep voice and shut the fuck up. Don't talk first. It will be uncomfortable.

- Have clear processes for them to hire you.

- Speak to each person like they're going to hire you. Speak like this: "When you hire me, this is how we will work together."

- Make it easy for them to pay you; don't create difficult processes or barriers to hiring you.

- However they want to pay— "That sounds great" and make sure to set up that payment method.

- Before doing your pitch, ask them about their pain points; do your pitch, but include how the things you do help them overcome their pain points.

- Don't sell; show a massive amount of value.

- Provide specific solutions to their problems.

- Have emotional intelligence; if they're not buying, figure out the barriers and overcome them.

- Ask them, "What is preventing you from moving forward?"

- Offer a 30-minute complimentary workshop or session, contingent upon what you do. Show people how valuable you are.

- Are you blaming yourself for everything so you can improve? "If you want to make two times more money, make yourself two times as valuable" —Jim Rohn

How To Run a Business Meeting

Before The Meeting:

- Set up your calendar (Calendly) for availability. For example, six 30-minute meetings on Thursdays and Fridays.

- Don't do phone calls.

- Make sure that Calendly, Zoom, and Google Calendar are all integrated.

- Make sure your Calendly automatically creates a Zoom call and places it on your Google Calendar.

- Make sure your Calendly sends texts and e-mails one day before and one hour before the meeting.

- Craft an intake form for when people set meetings. Make sure that it captures the information you will need, such as their name, phone number, email address, LinkedIn URL, website URL, why they want to meet, what barriers they're facing, and where they see themself in six months.

- Have the questions that will help you close a deal, not run a project. Do you get that? Ask me about it.

- Research the people you are meeting with for 30 minutes the day before the meeting. (See Researching People page for more details)

Day Of the Meeting:

- Refresh your memory before the meeting by looking at their profiles again.

- Open their LinkedIn page and Website for easy access during the meeting.

During The Meeting:

- Establish rapport in the first minute.

- Add value in the second minute. Add value in the first two minutes by giving feedback on how they are marketing themselves: "May I give you feedback on some things?"

- Ask them to pitch you for eight minutes.

- SHUT UP AND ACTIVELY LISTEN! Take short handwritten notes while they're talking. Write down what they're looking for so you can incorporate it into your pitch.

- After they speak for 8 minutes, take control:

    o Say: "Cool", or "Got it", and "Let me tell you what I do".

      Do your 8-minute pitch, incorporating your specific solutions to their specific problems.

    o When they ask the price— This is the signal that they're ready to buy and it's time to close. Tell them your price confidently and SHUT UP!

    o Ask for the sale even if they don't ask for your price but you believe they're a qualified lead (someone with the money and desire for your product).

- Handle objections if their face is scrunched up and they're not ready to buy. You're really asking them to tell you how to close the deal.

    o Say, "I thought this was what you needed. What pain point am I not hitting?" or "What barriers are we facing" or "Well, this is why you said you needed me. You don't want to be in the same spot 6 months from now, do you?"

    o Listen to what they say.

In General:

- People will be lying to you most of the time. They're not intentionally lying, they're simply not honest with themselves.

- Closes can happen at any time. As soon as you hear, "How much is that," you tell them your price and shut up.

    o You have to take the money out of their pocket and put it in your pocket.

    o It's VERY IMPORTANT that you close now while they're still emotional and the decision has been made. NO EXCUSES!

    o If they leave the meeting without buying, all they will have is negative thoughts about why they shouldn't buy.

    o When they want to pay you, take their money and say thank you!

- 100% of my clients are successful when they listen and take action on what they learn from me.

Researching People

Research is an emotional and professional investment.

Benefits of Research:

- Strengthens pitches

- Adds value

- Communicates interest

- Evokes familiarity

- Makes you look good:

- Communicates high social-intelligence

- Distinguishes you from others

- Improves engagement and communication

How to Research:

- Set aside about 30 minutes 1-2 days before the meeting

- Visit their LinkedIn profile and take note of:

  o Posts and recent activity

  o What they're working on

  o Shared connections

  o Education and Work History

  o Recommendations (given and received)

  o Values and beliefs (Vision, Mental Health Awareness, Work-Life Balance, etc.)

  o Anything fun/recreational (hobbies, interests, etc.)

- Visit their other online contact points:

  o Website

- o Social Media (Facemanual, Instagram, YouTube, etc.)
- o Watch their videos and listen to their podcasts

Check Your Research:

- Can you clearly communicate what it is they do?
- Do you know what they're working on in terms of important projects?
- Are you familiar with their network, groups, and shared connections?
- Do you understand what is emotionally relevant to them (work-life balance, mental health, etc.)?
- Do you have a shortlist of meaningful questions to ask them?
- Is there a sense of familiarity, camaraderie, and connection during the meeting?

Pre-Meeting Calendar Form Example

(Asterisk* indicates a required question)

Name *

Email *

Please share anything that will help prepare for our meeting. *

Why did you decide to meet with me? What do you hope to gain from our complimentary session? *

What is your website URL? *

Please connect with me on LinkedIn. Please don't just show me the link to your LinkedIn. Please connect with me. https://www.linkedin.com/in/sajadahusain/ *

What is your biggest hurdle right now? *

Wave a magic wand and fast forward six months down the line. What would outrageous success look like then? *

Are you currently working full-time on your business? If not, why not? *
(Give the prospect a task to invest in you, such as a YouTube video or podcast to listen to)

Bonus! Please listen to this with your full attention. If you do, I'll know you're serious about doing business with me, in one capacity or another.

Thank you.
https://www.youtube.com/watch?v=5EPA3hGj3h0 *

And finally!!!! How did you find me? *

CHAPTER SIX:
THE CAPSTONE: THE THREE
KEYS TO SUCCESS

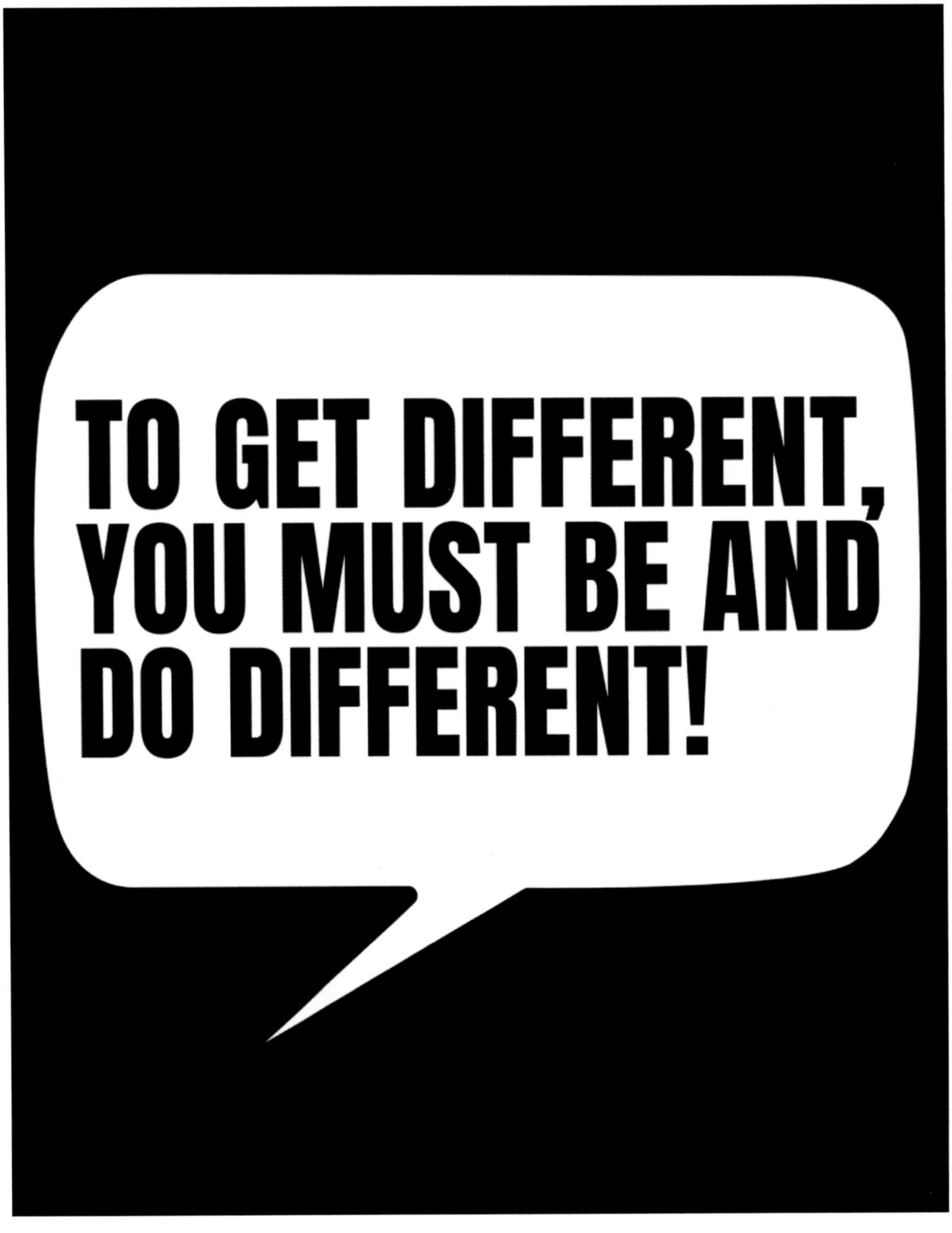
TO GET DIFFERENT, YOU MUST BE AND DO DIFFERENT!

Chapter six discusses the entrepreneurial mentality.

You have officially made it to the final chapter!

We're going to talk about the three keys to success.

What are the three keys to success?

Now you know how to close. You know how to set up and run business meetings, you have got your pitch down, and you should be rockin' and rollin'. You know your plan and you know your numbers.

What do you need to focus on now?

You have been doing this throughout what you have learned.

Number one: *Persistence.*

Keep going and going and going no matter what, but you want to be stubborn, but not stupid stubborn.

I had a client who loved socializing so she didn't take time to do her paperwork. Make sure that if you love socializing, you create time for administrative work.

I also had a client who spent 90% of his time on his website. Think about the things you've been avoiding and that you're still avoiding.

Think about the things that have been on your schedule that keep getting pushed to the next day or the next week and make sure that you are focusing on all aspects of your business.

Number two: *Sacrifice.*

Giving up something to get something. The more you want to get rid of something else, the more you have to give up what you've got.

You've been working 12 hours a day, productive hours, seven days a week for the last six weeks. That really can't change. This isn't a six-week boot camp.

I lied to you and now you don't get to find out until right now.

This is a lifestyle. This is a mindset.

It doesn't have to be the 12 hours necessarily. But if you start slacking off on the scheduling, you start slacking off on the number of hours you put in... you're going to get out what you put in.

Even when you are done reading this manual, you need to be doing all of this for yourself.

Stay consistent.

My clients who are very successful, which is most of them, continue to operate in this way.

As soon as you take your foot off the gas, everything goes to hell.

One of my clients started taking off on Saturdays. She did that two weeks out of my program. She told me what happened was that not only was Saturday messed up then...so was Sunday, Monday Tuesday, Wednesday, and Thursday. She was getting two productive days a week by taking one day off per week.

Stick to it and continue to sacrifice if this is really what you want.

Check out the Eric Thomas video: "How bad do you want it?"

You need to stay on your own ass even though I'm not going to be there to be on you.

Number Three: *Organization.*

Finally, organization means structure, logistics, protocols, and processes.

At this point, you have a process of how to research people, you have a process for how to create a strategy, and you have a process of how to close a deal. Your clients have processes for what it looks like when they work with you. What most of my clients say is they have many processes for many different things, even grocery shopping.

Continue to develop those processes, especially if you want to take this from being self-employed if that's where you're at in your business as a solo practitioner to being a business owner, where you're no longer working in your business.

You only work on your business.

You have staff, contractors, employees, and managers that are running it. You're going to need SOPs, standard operating procedures, for everything that you do in your business, so you can say here's what I do.

Do this, take it, and run with it.

That's how you will be able to bring on contractors and staff and get it to the point where you're no longer working. Basically, you're making money without working and that requires massive organization.

I don't give a shit about other people's opinions.

People's opinions don't matter. Opinions are like assholes, and everybody has one. A lot of people's opinions are wrong. The moon is not made of green cheese.

At the bottom of the mountain, there are a lot of people. The higher up you climb the mountain, the more difficult it's going to become. When you get to the top of the mountain, you're going to have a lot of people talking shit about you.

The universe is going to test you.

This happens to my clients.

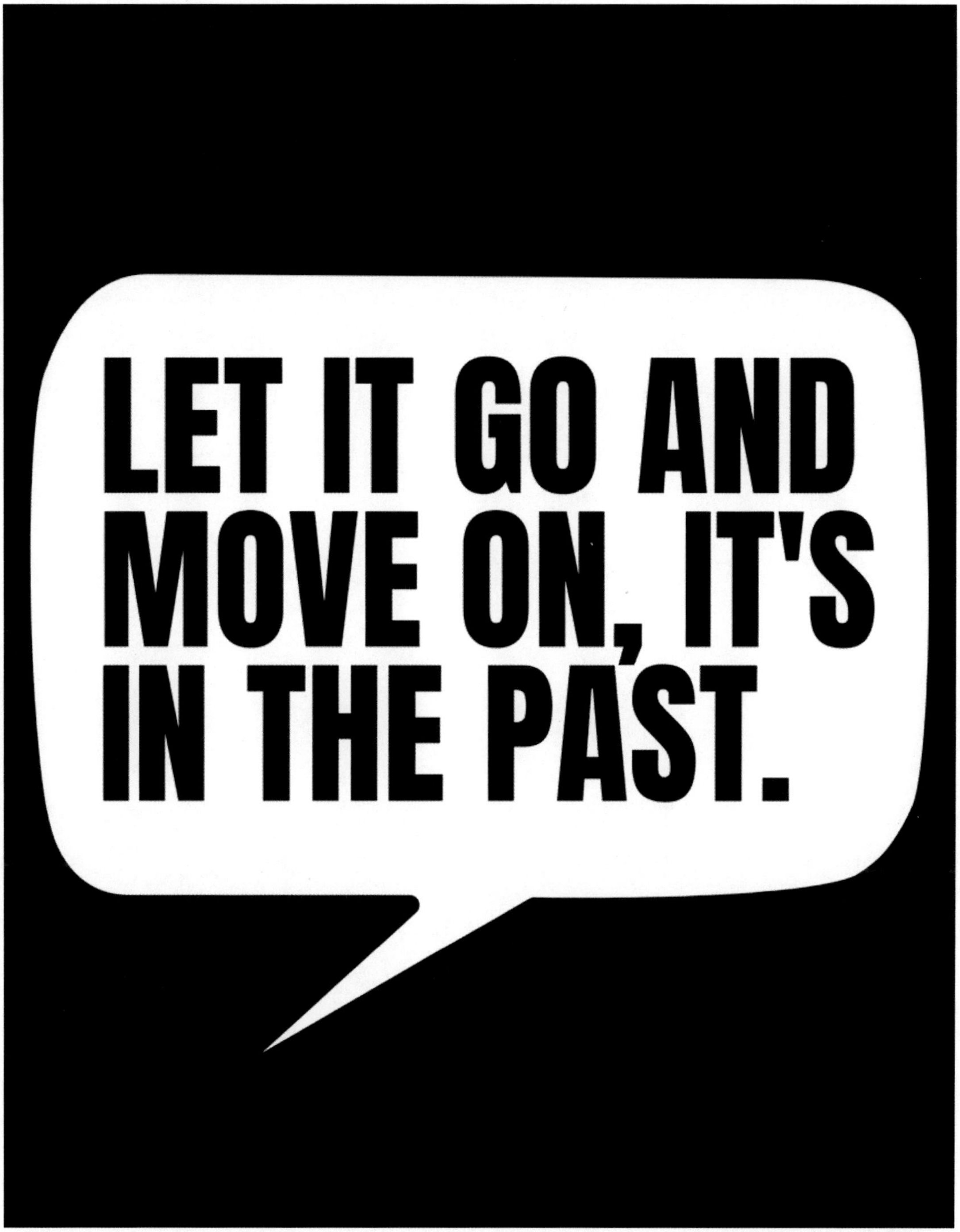
LET IT GO AND MOVE ON, IT'S IN THE PAST.

One of my clients put something in my online community about wanting to give up. Les Brown says most people give up at the one yard line. I asked her to call me, and she called me.

I was talking to her about the lady who wrote the Harry Potter series. I don't know if these numbers are exactly correct, but I believe she went to seventeen publishers.

I believe she was turned down by all seventeen publishers. She's a billionaire now.

My client said, "I've got this really big deal I'm not getting, and they won't even get back to me." She's a Black female. She said, "They're going to the white men or the white women. They're not even giving me a chance." Then, I told the Harry Potter story. She said, "It's been four months, and they haven't gotten back to me. I've contacted him several times."

While I'm telling her the Harry Potter story. She goes, "Hold on Sajad. You're not going to believe this!" They emailed her back right then.

As soon as you're ready to quit, it could be in that moment where the breakthrough occurs, and you get that big deal.

You've got to maintain the faith.

You've got to believe it's going to happen.

You've got to have positive thinking.

You're not operating out of blind belief because you have a plan.

You have ROI, you have CAC, you have a strategy, you can show massive value, and you can negotiate and close deals. Probably by now, you have way more self-confidence, because you've been learning from me.

You are building a network of people around you. You have relationships with plenty of people. Your calendar is booked out for the next two or three weeks or two to three months by now.

Don't get disheartened at any point. Because once you start doing that, you're fucking yourself.

Always the darkest before the light.

You will get tested as soon as you're about to sell a big deal. One of my clients was working on a deal, I think a $120 million deal. Her software goes down. Right? That's a fucking test. Absolutely.

How bad do you want it?

You can quit and you can get a job…

Entrepreneurship sucks. I tell people that before they hire me. It's mostly failure. That's not an excuse for my program.

That's what sales is. That's what entrepreneurship is. That is what business is.

JUST GET TO WORK. STOP BEING A LAZY FUCKING CRYIN' ASS BITCH.

You still have to have a great attitude.

You never know who is going to buy.

You don't make the decision for them.

In entrepreneurship, when you meet with somebody, you think, "They're definitely going to hire me!"

Then they don't hire you and you have the exact solution to their problem.

The coolest part of entrepreneurship is when you don't anticipate them hiring you at all. You think they're just meeting with you to shoot the shit and sell their bullshit and then they hire you!

You can't decide for them.

Just trust and follow the fucking process.

You are reading this manual because what you were doing was not working before.

Do not go back to what you were doing before.

What were you doing?

You were ruminating, you were meditating, learning, reading, and you were analyzing. You were doing program development. You were creating things. You had impostor syndrome. You weren't taking massive action.

It's 95% action and 5% analysis.

Take massive fucking action.

Don't go back to that shit you did before you read this manual.

And if you do that, don't say my program doesn't work. Because it's not a six-week program. Take a look at the results.

Why should you continue to do what you've been doing?

Look at what the fuck this has gotten you so far. Keep going. Keep doing what you have been doing.

Look at it like working out. Yeah, people go get a gym membership.

They go and work out and they start to see results. Then they go back to what they were doing before.

All of a sudden, there comes the weight, there comes the unhealthy and it's all because they quit doing what was giving them results in the first place because they wanted it to be easier, when it was easier before.

There's no easy way out of this.

There's no better way.

Don't chase the shiny fucking objects. I'm not saying that my way is the only way. It may or may not be the best way. I know it is a way that definitely works. When people stick with it. You have to stick with it.

The gym analogy or metaphor, I always confuse those two words. I think that's from coming from immigrant parents. There's some things I still don't understand yet…

Lazy people say yeah, "When you are working out, you still take a day off."

What happens in business is, if you take a day off, you don't lose just that day. The consequences of that day off are exponential. You take three days off or you take a week off. You've lost all that momentum.

You have got to keep the momentum going.

When you have momentum going, you are in a state of flow.

When you stop, think of how hard it is to get back into it. Now you're trying to push a rock up a hill, right? Just like with working out, people say, "Yeah, I'll take a day off." If you take a day off of working out, the next day is three times as hard, if not harder.

Every time I take a day off from working out, it's six months later, then it takes three weeks to build back up.

Just think about all the great shit you have going on right now.

This happens for everyone. 100% of my clients have great shit going on.

At this point, you have got what you got because of what you put in. If you stop doing that, you're going to start seeing different results. You got the great results you're getting because of what you've been doing.

Podcasts, networking events, presentations, social media posts, you've been doing those every day. Some of my clients will start slowing down, doing fewer LinkedIn posts, doing fewer TikToks, and doing less social media. They start going back to program creation.

They start doing things their own way again.

They go back to creating because that is what's fun and easy for them.

You need a mixture of all those things. Some people just do social media posts, and they think that people are going to come out of the woodwork and by not having conversations or not actually talking to people, how do you expect to close deals?

Dear Future Client,

You already know what to do. You've been doing it. You have to keep doing it. If you take your foot off the gas, it's not going to just go slower. It's going to fall off the fucking rails. So, keep doing what you're doing. Don't stop, push through. Embrace the suck and congratulations on completing the sixth chapter.

Thank you for the opportunity to share my knowledge with you!

Entrepreneur Mentality

Would you let an employee behave the way you are, or accept the excuses you're telling yourself?

The Three Keys to Success
1. **Persistence**: Keep going no matter what, be stubborn but not stupid stubborn, and persist logically.
2. **Sacrifice**: Giving up something to get something else.
   The more you want to get one thing, the more you have to give up other things.
3. **Organization**: Structure, logistics, protocol, and processes. Make every second count.

- Be stubborn but not stupid stubborn.
- Entrepreneurship is hard work and mostly failure and rejection.
- Entrepreneurs do all the jobs, including the ones they don't like!
- Failure for an entrepreneur is when they quit trying.
- Rejections are opportunities to learn how to do things better.
- Learn, grow, and evolve.

People's opinions of you don't matter.

Don't pay attention to the failures. It's all a win when you learn something from it.

SUMMARY

Content Covered

How to Create and Stick to a Schedule

Branding & Pitching: Emotional Connect, Packages, & Processes

Quantifiable Measurements: Activity does not equal productivity, ROI, CAC, where are you spending time/what are you getting back

Mapping: Personal & Professional Nut/what are you forgetting, know your goal, what is the plan, smaller goals/action steps/due dates/milestones, what needs to get done by when, how are you quantifiable measuring success, be logical and number focused

Loose Ends: You have more than a million questions to ask me when you hire me

Negotiations & Closing Deals: Always take yes for an answer, when they're ready to buy shut your mouth and take the money, it's all about value, overcoming barriers, and addressing pain points

Entrepreneurial Mentality: The 3 Keys to Success - persistence, sacrifice, organization, To-Do List, habits/behaviors/character, structure is freedom, organization is the opposite of chaos

Appendix: Pictures of some of my 163 Bitches. My lawyers have advised me that I can't show pics of my bitches in my manual. When you hire me, I'll text them to you.

TESTIMONIALS

"After working for others for thirty years and feeling tired of it, I decided to break free and do something more entrepreneur-ish. Instead of starting my own business, I began working as a 1099 contractor for a one-person web development company. I also created an LLC in case I wanted to expand to provide sales services for other businesses.

I initially worked closely with the web developer to get sales going for his business. Aside from learning his process, a significant change for me was that I was now selling to small companies despite having a B2B sales background in acquiring larger clients. It was overwhelming, along with the anxiousness of not receiving a regular paycheck.

Due to COVID-19, we were still in a virtual world. I tried cold calling for a bit but followed the lead of the web developer and took part in several virtual networking groups. These online networking meetings were filled with people selling various products and services - everything from anti-aging products to life coaching to people calling themselves Medicare savings experts.

I was under the impression these folks were ripe for multi-page websites or social media management, but the truth was, most of them were like me, trying to find their way, and were broke.

So, while attending these Hollywood Square-style networking events, I heard networking hosts preaching, "We're not here to sell". When it was time to give our 30-second commercial, I did some weird-ass sing-songy shit that made people wonder, "What does this guy actually do?"

Then, when we broke into "breakout rooms", I followed the advice to get to know, like, and trust people, and we talked about family, the weather, and a bunch of other bullshit.

Then one day, I came across a new networking group, where I listened to Sajad call out the horse hockey that was making us all soft.

He said, "It's stupid not to pitch. No, you're not going to pressure people, but instead, be clear on what you do and give away massive value in your consults and one-to-one meetings. Show your expertise, but don't be passive. And treat one-to-one meetings as business meetings."

Sajad practiced exactly what he preached, giving nuggets of entrepreneurial advice in these networking groups that differed from the let's be friends approach. I started to follow his daily social media posts, and each time, he gave more helpful advice on how to be a fearless, productive entrepreneur. Ultimately, I entered his six-week boot camp program.

I knew he was going to kick my butt, but I also knew that's exactly what I needed. The skills he taught me were detailed and practical, and because I now had systems in place for time management, understanding the value of my time, and running successful business meetings to close more business, I gained a much stronger belief in my ability.

Furthermore, I achieved a new level of responsibility that I had never before held when he aided me in realizing that I was deceiving myself about the amount of effort I was putting in. My sales numbers immediately saw an improvement, but the increased sense of self-worth and bravery gave me the motivation to become my own business owner.

As a result, I established my own marketing agency, The Right Path Marketing.

Eighteen months after completing his boot camp and thirteen months since starting Right Path, I'm closing contracts worth 3-4x more than I did as a contractor for the small web developer with double the margins, along with recurring revenues from ongoing services.

Furthermore, the courage I gained has helped me in other areas of my life, including my relationships with friends and family and setting boundaries to, as Sajad would say, "Be the pimp, not the whore!!!"

-Scott Humphries, CEO, The Right Path Marketing

"I was actually referred to Sajad after five months of my contracts turned into three weeks' worth of work. Ouch.

Our first meeting was in the afternoon, and I was at the gym. I ran out to make sure I was on-time. He was sitting in front of a blacked out screen, smoking a cigarette. His first words…

"This guy is in his fucking car! Who do you think I am?"

"Well, you said you don't reschedule."

"You're right. It'd be the first and last time you were ever late to one of my meetings."

This shit was hilarious. It was right up my alley. He knew how to sell me because he understands how to listen and tailor the pitch to exactly what the client's pain points are. Mine being that I was good at Supply Chain Operations, but short of submitting a resume, I had no clue how to generate my own work as a Supply Chain Consultant.

He instantly pitched my own services back to me and said, "I just bullshit pitched better than you and I'm not even in your industry."

That did not hurt my feelings at all. That's what I needed. Somebody who made entrepreneurship a science rather than an art.

I was the worst at LinkedIn posting. He said it and I was.

It took me 2.5 weeks to get my pitch right. He said, "You haven't given me the same pitch twice, yet. You're too smart. Even when you dumb it down, you're still too smart. It needs to be on a 6th grade level."

Pissed only at myself, I talked to myself on a plane flight.

Imagining explaining what I do to my kids and then typing my pitch. I delivered the pitch that night. He said "Nice." I read the pitch to keep from messing up. The second night, reading the pitch got in my way.

I knew my pitch…

High

Drunk

Coming out of a coma

You can drop me ANYWHERE in my pitch.

And I can walk you back to the beginning or all the way to the end.

My emotional connect used to suck, now I know how to tap into my 24 years of Supply Chain industry experience to speak to pain points I know my prospects are facing because I've faced them at every place I've ever been.

I know what the Big Dogs do well. I know what the Big Dogs can do better. I share that with the Small and Medium Dogs looking to become the NEXT Medium and Big Dogs.

I've never had this much structure for my own organization and it is life changing. I used to work 12 hour days incessantly for other companies. Now I work 12 hour days for my business, on the business just as much as in the business.

There have been MANY people that have never liked or commented on a post but have mentioned that they follow and enjoy my content daily. I have a good problem. I'm exceeding the capacity for what I can do on my own.

I'm HAVING to add people to Xpandur, LLC. Because I learned how to prospect, I stay top of mind with referrals coming in from contacts even months after we talked.

Insane.

I can talk to C-Suite confidently and succinctly describing exactly how to solve fundamental pain points of "Getting Warehouses MORE thruput with the SAME hours." 30-second, 1-minute, 2-minute, 4-minute, and full 8-minute pitch all nailed down.

I asked God for guidance with Xpandur, LLC. He sent that guidance through Sajad. This was no coincidence."

-Adrian Betts, Operations Consultant, Xpandur, LLC

"When I hired Sajad, I was making about $30K a year as a freelance artist, struggling to figure out how to start a business and move from scarcity mode—though I wouldn't have admitted that at the time—to becoming a successful entrepreneur with a six-figure income that's still growing.

What I appreciated the most about his training was that he was relentless in his approach. He has a loud bark and a huge heart, and if you just followed and implemented what he said, there was definitely growth. My biggest takeaways from working with Sajad were having a strong mindset and being intentional with every meeting, networking event, and opportunity.

If you are someone who is willing to do the work, not take shit personally, and be consistent, then you will succeed in his program.

If you enter Cause & Effect knowing that you will be receiving a boot-camp-like approach to development and growth, then you will leave the program with renewed confidence. If not, then you will struggle.

I have always been drawn to the unconventional, so this program worked for me. It wasn't just about business growth; it was about transforming my perspective."

~ Meridith Grundei, Founder of Grundei Coaching and Confidently Speaking

"In the year following working with Sajad, I increased my business income by 5x, left my 18 year corporate healthcare career, and ended my 18 year relationship, one day after another.

After successfully surviving his program, I now have Sajad as an ongoing mentor and now a business partner. Massive opportunity has come my way from thinking and believing differently, which turns into KNOWING.

Being called out for living in a victim mentality and learning I was a people-pleaser who was too "nice" for business, was the best thing that has ever happened to me in my life.

I learned to love and respect myself again, regained my confidence, set the bar higher for myself, and raised my standards for who I choose to surround myself with to do all I am set out to do personally and professionally.

-Jen Carpenter, Secure & Savvy Solutions

ABOUT THE AUTHOR

I will beat you with a big ass stick, you will hate me for 6 weeks and be in love with me in four months from now. After that, we might be friends.

I'm pretty much happy all of the time. I am kind, humble, brilliant, and extremely good-looking. I own a $76k Twin Turbo, a 4 bedroom two bathroom house in Chicago that's paid off in cash, and a mountain in Arizona…It's called Mount Sajad! I offend, repulse, and attract the right people. This saves me from wasting time. You are the problem…you need to take responsibility and get out of your own way. A dream without a plan is a wish, you need a strategy. I'm so dope!

-Sajad Abid Husain, Esq

"Insanity is doing the same thing over and over again and expecting different results." - Albert Einstein.

CAUSE AND EFFECT CONSULTING IS CHANGING THE WORLD!!!!!

Sajad Husain, Esq. is a persevering, enterprising, and top-performing executive and former attorney with expertise in vision-setting, project oversight, development, and implementation, compliance, internal and external communications, relationship management, legal and policy review, resource, and people management, community outreach, and organizing.

He is an analytical and broad-minded influencer focused on solving problems, mediating disputes, and resolving matters to ensure ultimate project success.

Sajad is a highly sought-after mentor, coach, and sounding board for ideas and key advising.